MORE from JOE HILL:

LOCKE & KEY
- *Welcome to Lovecraft*
- *Head Games*
- *Crown of Shadows*
- *Keys to the Kingdom*
- *Clockworks*
- *Alpha & Omega*

THE CAPE

THE CAPE: 1969

WRAITH

THUMBPRINT

20th CENTURY GHOSTS

HEART-SHAPED BOX

HORNS

NOS4A2

THE FIREMAN

JOE HILL
TALES FROM THE
DARKSIDE
SCRIPTBOOK

Become our fan on Facebook **facebook.com/idwpublishing**
Follow us on Twitter **@idwpublishing**
Subscribe to us on YouTube **youtube.com/idwpublishing**
See what's new on Tumblr **tumblr.idwpublishing.com**
Check us out on Instagram **instagram.com/idwpublishing**

ISBN : 978-1-63140-725-3   19 18 17 16   1 2 3 4

COVER ART BY
CHARLES PAUL WILSON III

PUBLISHED BY
TED ADAMS

COLLECTION DESIGN BY
RICHARD SHEINAUS
FOR **GOTHAM DESIGN**

SPECIAL THANKS TO
RISA KESSLER
JOHN VAN CITTERS
AND
SEAN DAILEY
FOR THEIR INVALUABLE
ASSISTANCE

IDW Publishing does not read or accept unsolicited submissions of ideas, stories, or artwork.

Ted Adams, CEO & Publisher
Greg Goldstein, President & COO
Robbie Robbins, EVP/Sr. Graphic Artist
Chris Ryall, Chief Creative Officer/Editor-in-Chief
Matthew Ruzicka, CPA, Chief Financial Officer
Dirk Wood, VP of Marketing
Lorelei Bunjes, VP of Digital Services
Jeff Weber, VP of Licensing, Digital and Subsidiary Rights
Jerry Bennington, VP of New Product Development

For international rights, please contact licensing@idwpublishing.com

Tales From the Darkside created by George Romero.

JOE HILL
TALES FROM THE DARKSIDE
SCRIPTBOOK

SCRIPTS written by
JOE HILL

ILLUSTRATIONS by
CHARLES PAUL WILSON III

EDITED by
JUSTIN EISINGER

IDW

Getting in Touch with My Darkside

by Joe Hill

SOMEONE—maybe the show-runner Joshua Friedman—said screenwriters are professional scribblers who dislike being alone even more than they dislike writing.

I had been alone for a long time and wanted to be part of a team, wanted to enlist in someone's squadron. I missed people.

I had people once, comrades-in-arms, when I was writing the scripts for a thirty-seven issue comic book series, *Locke & Key*. Sometimes, when I'm asked about being a comic book writer, I say it's the closest I'll ever come to knowing what it must be like to be in a rock band. Gabriel Rodriguez, who illustrated the series, beginning to end, was the lead guitarist and I was the drummer. He made the music; I found the beat. Robbie Robbins, who lettered all the word balloons and put the **POW** in our *KA-POW*, was obviously our vocalist. Jay Fotos, the colorist, created feeling in much the same way a keyboardist will provide emotional coloration to a song. Chris Ryall, who edited *Locke & Key*, played a role similar to producers like George Martin or Jeff Lynne: he was there every step of the way to pull our mess of ideas into tight focus, to hack our eleven-minute jam sessions into hummable three-minute singles.

Then we made the last issue and it was all done.

I went away and wrote a book and it took a long time and I began to wonder what other human beings were like. Right around then, a producer named Mitchell Galin sent me a note to ask if I wanted to write the pilot episode for a relaunch of the 1980s horror show *Tales From the Darkside*. Half-hour format, twenty-four page script, just like writing a comic book.

I had (and continue to have) an author boner for TV. By now you've probably read at least one article explaining how the best modern television shows—"The Americans," "Stranger Things," "Orange Is the New Black"—have been composed like Victorian novels, with all the complexities and depth we expect from sprawling works of literature. It's true. In fact, it's so true, the tide has begun to flow the other way, and modern novels have increasingly begun to feel more like cable TV. My own last book, *The Fireman*, was very consciously modeled on the structure of a prestige cable show. It was broken into nine distinct episodes, each with its own beginning, middle, and end, all of which connected together to tell a single larger overarching narrative. TV-style storytelling was already very much on my mind when Mitchell reached out to me. I was ready to say *yes* before he even asked.

But even if I had been less inclined to accept a TV job, I think *Darkside* would've pulled me in. Because blood calls to blood.

DID YOU EVER SEE the original *Tales From the Darkside*, with its famously portentous opening narration by Vincent Price?

> *"Man lives in the sunlit world of what he believes to be reality.* **But**... *there is... unseen by most, an underworld... a place that is just as real, but not as brightly lit... a* **Darkside***."*

Except, of course, the narrator wasn't really Vincent Price, or even a guy who sounded much like him. The original show was too cheap to afford a Vincent Price. Go back and watch a couple of those old episodes (or better yet, don't). Most of them look like they were filmed on home video cameras in your mom's kitchen.

Yet a few of those old *Tales* retain the power to disturb and inspire, largely due to the artistic cunning of the creators who worked on the show. Jodie Foster cut her teeth as a director on *Darkside*. Bob Balaban took a turn behind the camera. George Romero, Tom Savini, Robert Bloch, Clive Barker, and Tom Monteleone all turned in contributions.

My dad even wrote a couple. Yeah.

I won't go into the whole story of how I tried to avoid being known as Stephen King's son. It's been well documented elsewhere. I'll just say that as a young writer, I felt it would be a disaster to publish as Joseph King, because inevitably my work would be judged against my father's and I would fail to measure up. (I was right about that, by the way. I don't. But then again—who does?)

So in the late 90s I began to try to sell short stories under the name Joe Hill and kept it quiet about my family. Eventually, after a decade, my pen name fell apart and the truth came out, but by then I had written some good shorts, sold a collection, and broke in over at Marvel with an eleven-page *Spider-Man* comic. Most importantly, my pseudonym gave me the cover I needed to build up my confidence, and by the time it was all over, I had settled into my own skin. If I am not Stephen King (and I am not), it turned out I had it in me to be an acceptable Joe Hill. That seems to be good enough.

The best thing about being publicly outed as Stephen King's son is now I can acknowledge how much I love his stories (and him). Every artist is a sculptor. The lives they've lived and their creative influences are their only clay. As it happens, my father's stories are my biggest influences. And because he is a loving, caring, thoughtful parent, who has been with me every step of the way, he's also an outsize part of my personal experiences. To try and write as if he didn't have a place in my life would be an act of self-abnegation far larger than taking a pen name. It would also, to my mind anyway, be a little gross. If I was eager to give into my *Darkside*, then, it was because I knew my dad was waiting there for me. Blood calls to blood.

As it happened, my father had scripted one of the very best episodes of *Tales From the Darkside*, a story titled "Word Processor of the Gods." It was a thing about a homemade computer that can rewrite reality. Bruce Davidson starred and helped to vault the material over the hurdle of a microscopic budget. I loved that story as a child and, gradually, I began to see it as the key to a completely reinvented show.

I imagined a series of standalone weird tales which would always begin with a reality-warping "Darkside Event." Lives would be demolished and rebuilt by these intrusions of the fantastic. Gradually, over the course of the first season, it would become clear that the Darkside Events all sprang from the same source: a crippled psychic with a microprocessor in his brain, a device called a Darkside Amplifier, which has given his monstrous Id the powers of a petulant god. In time, some of those who had been touched by the Darkside would band together in a desperate play to set the universe right again.

I was hired to write a single episode, but got carried away by my own concept (Mine? Or my father's?). Originally the show was meant to be a half-hour long, like the original. I wrote one twenty-four-page script, then another. The production team decided to weld both stories into one night of television and make *Darkside* an hour long. I wrote a third script, this one a fifty-minute episode, which would establish the underlying mythology of the entire show. That one, "Black Box," was the best of them, I think. To polish things off, I turned in a series Bible for three seasons of television.

We filmed the first two standalones, "A Window Opens" and "Sleepwalker," in Vancouver, in the early spring of 2015. Brad Buecker directed with the lazy confidence and athletic prowess of a professional surfer. There were some test screenings, everyone loved it, and *Tales From the Darkside* went on to have seven hit seasons in my imagination.

In real life, though, the CW passed.

I can't tell you why we didn't get on the air. Maybe, in the end, the whole thing wound up too big for its own britches, was wildly too ambitious, and way beyond what CBS thought they signed up for.

I can't complain. IDW Publishing won the rights to adapt my scripts as a series of comic books. Chris Ryall got the band back together—the whole *Locke & Key* team—and produced some delightfully trippy issues. I got out of my office and saw people and had some fun and no one made me give the money back.

Then it was over and I returned to my office and worked on some novellas until I began to miss people again. Right around then, Ted Adams, the CEO of IDW, called me up to talk about his company's expansion into television. They had just landed a hit show on SyFy with *Wynonna Earp* and were searching for a follow-up. Ted thought of *Locke & Key* and was wondering if I had any interest in writing a pilot…

— Joe Hill
London, September 2016

A WINDOW OPENS

DARKSIDE PILOT—EPISODE 1: "A WINDOW OPENS"

FADE IN:

ACT I

1   INT. JOSS' CAR—DAY   1

JOSS, a cute grad student, has one hand on the wheel and the other on her smartphone. She's up to that great bad habit of the 21st century: texting while she drives. John Cafferty's "On the Darkside" blasts from the radio.

2   EXT. SUBURBAN PARADISE—ROAD—CONTINUOUS   2

Joss' car speeds through a housing development familiar from a half dozen eighties-era Spielberg films: a zone of bright green yards, bright blue skies, and bright big futures. A sound rises, electrical in nature, a little like that drone of feedback at the start of The Beatles' "I Feel Fine."

3   INT. JOSS' CAR—CONTINUOUS   3

With "Darkside" blasting, Joss doesn't hear that building drone. With her eyes fixed on her smartphone, she doesn't see the color leeching out of the neighborhood around her, everything taking on the monochrome tint of a photo negative.

4   EXT. SUBURBAN PARADISE—ROAD—CONTINUOUS   4

A bright lump appears in the road, a glowing form in the shape of a kneeling man. The sound builds to a deafening whine. *Time locks in place.*

Joss' car freezes, rushing right toward the man in the road—which resolves at last into a grizzled young guy with the grooming habits of a hobo. This is NEWMAN and if DARKSIDE has a hero, he's it. Too bad he'll be dead by the first commercial break.

Newman rises to his feet, bleary and confused. He casts his gaze around, trying to orient himself, and has time to turn his head and stare into Joss' unmoving car... twenty feet away.

(CONTINUED)

5   INT. JOSS' CAR—CONTINUOUS   5

Joss stares back, horrified, her phone sliding out of her suddenly slack grip. Newman and Joss are the only two things in the scene that aren't frozen in time.

But not for long. In the next instant, *time comes unstuck.* The car lunges at Newman.

Joss wrenches at the wheel with a cry.

6   EXT. ROB/GLORIA'S HOUSE—CONTINUOUS   6

Joss's sunny little compact veers around Newman and clips someone's mailbox. Joss shrieks to a halt in front of a big new-built home. A realtor's sign stands in the front yard.

ANOTHER FAIRY-TALE HOME
SOLD BY MATHESON-JACKSON ESTATES...
wake up and live your dream!

Strawmen flank the front door, each in its own rocking chair: a mommy scarecrow and a daddy scarecrow, dusty and limp. Boxes in the driveway suggest a family just moving in. Newman isn't too upset he was almost run over, hardly seems to notice. He casts a wary glance at the just-sold home, then looks toward the other side of the road. There's another house being built over there, although right now it's little more than a muddy hole with a loader looming over it.

7   INT./EXT. JOSS' CAR—CONTINUOUS   7

Joss shudders behind the wheel, turns the car off. She takes a scared look over her shoulder for the guy she almost hit. We look with her—no one there. We come back to Joss and Newman is staring right through the window at her, too close.

                          NEWMAN
         You got trouble now, lady.

Joss shrieks.

                          JOSS
         Oh God! I'm so sorry. I didn't mean to—

                          NEWMAN
         Almost run me over?

                                                    (CONTINUED)

CONTINUED:

                    JOSS
—I'm so sorry. I don't know what just happened. Are
you all right?

                   NEWMAN
I'm not dead! Yet. It's still early. How about you? Let's
talk about you. What's your name?

                    JOSS
Joss Waldrop. This is my first time almost killing
someone and I feel really, really bad about it.

                   NEWMAN
Uh-huh. Uh-huh. Anything else you feel bad about?
Besides nearly running me down—do you have any
reason to be ashamed? Do you think you need to
repent for something?

Joss only stares, absorbing this—then gently locks her door. Not only is
Newman not offended, he beams at her.

                NEWMAN (CONT'D)
You don't have to be afraid of me. I'm on your side. I
will help you if you let me. And you *do* need help.
You're in trouble. This place is sick. Contaminated. It
was just blanketed by a Darkside Field and you drove
right into it. I'd tell you to run, but it's like passing
through radioactivity. You're charged now. You can't
run from a case of radiation poisoning. This crap
sticks to you. It's an appointment in Samarra.

                    JOSS
Appointment in *what*?

                   NEWMAN
Google it.

Joss looks away, her face comically alarmed. He's a crazy, obviously. She
begins to search through the mess around her.

NEWMAN (CONT'D)
What are you doing?

JOSS
Looking for my phone.

NEWMAN
I didn't mean Google it right now.

JOSS
I'm not! You seem very unhappy and I think you
could use some help. And I think I could use some
help too.

Newman bangs his head against her window in frustration, provoking
another shriek.

NEWMAN
No. Stop. You're in it now. I'm all the help you're
going to get. You might as well toss your phone into
the street.

JOSS
You're scaring me.

NEWMAN
Good! That's progress. Fear is a good thing. You want
to know what it's good for? Inspiration. And
awareness. You want to stay aware. Once you've been
marked by the Darkside, it's usually only a matter of
time before you're hunted down and made to answer
for something you've done. That's how this works.
And until you know what's coming for you, you have
to pay attention. Because this thing, it won't be
obvious. It's not just going to whistle and wave and—

A sharp whistle interrupts him.

8   EXT. CONSTRUCTION SITE—CONTINUOUS   8

The world's creepiest little boy stands beside the loader. This is WARD, a
child with hair the color of cobwebs. He has a tablet under one arm. He

(CONTINUED)

CONTINUED:

whistles a bit of the original *Tales From the Darkside* theme, waves, and strolls from view.

9   INT. JOSS' CAR—CONTINUOUS   9

Joss glances around to see what Newman is looking at, but can't spot the kid from her vantage point.

> NEWMAN
> Maybe I can stop this without anyone getting hurt.
> Besides me.

She watches him depart, moving toward the construction site. Joss finally digs her phone out of the mess and dials three numbers (guess which three). For a moment her thumb hovers over CALL. At last, though, she lowers the phone and shuts her eyes and exhales: it's over.

Bang bang bang! Newman raps on the passenger side window with one knuckle. Joss screams in a small voice.

> NEWMAN (CONT'D)
> You've got someone's mailbox under your front tire.

> Might want to move that before trying to go
> anywhere.

She watches him turn and amble on, vanishing beyond the loader. When he's well and gone, Joss steels herself and steps out of her car. Yep, there's the mailbox, right under her front driver's side tire.

10   EXT. ROB/GLORIA'S HOUSE—DAY   10

> JOSS
>
> Oh jeez.

Joss collects the mailbox and carries it up to the house. She passes between the two rocking chairs on the porch. They're empty now, no scarecrows to be seen. She rings the bell.

The door swings wide to reveal ROB, a Father-Knows-Best type. Farther down the hall we glimpse his wife, GLORIA, unpacking a box and hanging photos on the wall. Seems they just moved in. Both of them are dressed as the scarecrows were.

> ROB
>
> Hel-lo there! Everything all right?

Joss smiles bravely and holds up the crushed mailbox.

> JOSS
>
> Hi, I'm Joss Waldrop, I live about six blocks from here
> and I—
>
> (begins to cry)
>
> —I killed your mailbox. Yep! Welcome to the
> neighborhood.

> ROB
>
> Aw, kid! Are you all right? Gloria!

11   EXT. CONSTRUCTION SITE—DAY   11

Newman wanders around to the far side of the loader. A little girl sits on the treads, peering at a tablet with a glowing screen. Meet PAM, Ward's sister, and every bit as creepy.

Her tablet is as thin and beautiful as a sheet of stained glass. The branding on one side shows a demented sun: logo of the Brite*r*side Corporation.

(CONTINUED)

CONTINUED:

Beneath the screen, the tablet is identified as a LI'L WIN.

Ward stands a few steps from the edge of the enormous hole, looking through an identical tablet. He glances back to acknowledge Newman's presence.

                    WARD
          You were just lying in the road.

                    NEWMAN
          I know. I could've been killed, right? Not very safe. Of
          course, neither is playing on a construction site. I'm
          not sure your parents would think much of you being
          up here, kids.

                    WARD
          We're not hurting anyone.

                    PAM
          Not yet.

                    WARD
          Want to see our game?

                    NEWMAN
          Do I?

                              PAM
     Maybe she'd like to see!

Pam gestures with her head toward the house across the street.

LOOKING TOWARD ROB/GLORIA'S HOUSE:

From here we can see Joss, Gloria, and Rob in conversation on the front step.

                                             BACK TO...

Newman shakes his head.

                              NEWMAN
     Leave her out of it. Show me.

He approaches Ward to look at the boy's tablet.

THROUGH THE DEVICE:

The muddy hole, dusty boulders, stacks of lumber. A menu bar floats
over the view.

Ward has used his stylus to draw black tentacles on the screen so they
appear to be exploding from the giant hole. He taps them and they come to
life, lashing around. We HOLD on the tentacles for a moment, but when
Ward lowers the tablet there is, of course, nothing but an empty hole.

                    NEWMAN (CONT'D)
     Wow. Nice piece of tech.

                              PAM
     It's cutting edge.

                              WARD
     Now you go over by the hole and pretend it's getting
     you. The Bad Thing. And I'll take a picture. It'll be
     funny. It'll be so funny.

                              NEWMAN
     I don't think I like this game.

                              PAM
     I told you we should've showed the girl. He's no fun.

                              NEWMAN
     No! I'm fun! There's no need to bring her into this.

                                             (CONTINUED)

CONTINUED:

Newman creeps to the edge of the hole and looks into it. Empty.

WARD

Now turn around and look scared.

As Ward speaks he double taps THE BAD THING with the stylus. The screen reads: **RENDERING.**

Newman turns and tries on an unconvincing look of horror.

NEWMAN

How's that?

PAM	WARD
More scared!	More scared!

Newman tries one face and another. Tentacles uncoil from the hole behind him. At last he can hear them whipping about, which is when an expression of true terror crosses his face.

PAM & WARD

PERFECT!

The tentacles snarl around him.

12   EXT. ROB/GLORIA'S HOUSE—DAY   12

Under Rob and Gloria's ministrations, Joss has calmed herself. Gloria clutches a large framed photo of Ward and Pam, looking very Addams Family. Rob has taken the crushed mailbox off Joss's hands.

JOSS

I can't apologize—

GLORIA	ROB
Will you *stop*—	—Never you mind—

From across the street comes a choked cry. Joss jumps, looks around, but all the action is hidden behind the loader. Rob and Gloria must've heard that strangled shout, but their smiles remain fixed on their faces.

ROB (CONT'D)

Joss? Do you ever do babysitting?

JOSS

Pretty much every weekend since I was twelve.

ROB

No kidding...!

13   EXT. CONSTRUCTION SITE—DAY   13

Newman clutches the edge of the hole, ensnared by tentacles. The children gaze impassively down. Pam sketches something on her own tablet.

NEWMAN

You don't have to *do* this.

WARD

Of course we do. That's why we're here. And it's why *you're* here, too. *To start the story.* It's what you *always* do. You know that. You can start it and...

(gestures at the house)

...she can finish it.

In the background, a boulder sprouts pink, glittery wings, and begins to shimmy itself loose from the ground. The tentacles drag Newman out of sight, down into the hole, just as the boulder lifts itself into the air.

14   EXT. ROB/GLORIA'S HOUSE—DAY   14

Joss has turned back to look at Rob and Gloria, so she doesn't see the boulder rise into the air from behind the loader and hover on giant pink wings.

JOSS

I'm a grad student. We can always use a little extra money. I should do it for *free* after bashing your mailbox.

ROB

No, don't even think about it. This evening then?

JOSS

You bet.

Behind her, the boulder drops into the construction yard with a great **whump!** Joss spins, but there's nothing to see. After a moment, she looks

(CONTINUED)

CONTINUED:

back, trying to smile, but her eyes are bewildered. Gloria and Rob are unperturbed.

GLORIA

Can't wait for you to meet the kids.

ROB

They're going to have so much fun with you!

Joss grins uneasily.

15   EXT. CONSTRUCTION SITE—THE PIT—CONTINUOUS   15

The boulder lifts itself to reveal a dusty, bloody Newman, stamped down into a Newman-shaped impression in the dirt.

Shades of Loony Tunes here. He begins to flicker black-and-white, phasing out of the story. Newman covers his eyes.

NEWMAN

This is the third worst thing to happen to me all week.
(peeks through fingers)
Oh fuuuuuuuuu—

And the boulder drops again with a great big

SMASH CUT TO:

16   CREDITS: 16

Soft and sinister music that recalls the original *Tales From the Darkside* theme. We're looking at a glassy black cube with rotating sides. In each new facet we see another dizzying vision, yanked straight from your worst fever dreams. Newman speaks over the parade of appalling images.

> NEWMAN (V.O.)
> Most of us live in the sunlit world of what we *believe* to be reality. But there's another world—and you better hope it never touches you—bleeding through into our own. A *different* world that's not so brightly lit. **The Darkside** is rising, poisoning everything it touches... and it's my fault. Now I have to atone. Pray you never see me coming. There's a darkness following right behind me and if it finds you, you may never see the light again.

Images include:

A) a doll rots like a time-lapse reel of fruit going bad.

B) A trollish, blind child stacks a wall of blocks that read DIES DARK. He rearranges them to read DARKSIDE.

C) Newman's screaming face, eyes squeezed shut, tears of blood on his cheeks.

D) A crow lands on a street sign at the corner of BRADBURY and ROMERO. It flicks an impossible forked tongue at us.

E) A weird photo negative image of a grinning psychopath who bears a vague resemblance to Newman. His eyes are an irradiated blue; his teeth glow; his tie is a stripe of radioactive ash. Someday we will meet this awful fellow but not tonight...

The final facet turns to face us and we see in it Rob and Gloria's house at dusk...

ACT II

17   EXT. ROB/GLORIA'S HOUSE—MAGIC HOUR   17

The first stars show in an infernal sky. Laughter from in the house.

18   INT. ROB/GLORIA'S HOUSE—FRONT HALL—DUSK   18

Joss stands in the front hall, seeing Rob and Gloria off. Ward watches

(CONTINUED)

CONTINUED:

> from nearby, sitting on the stairs perhaps. Gloria has a purse, but sets it on an end table to get a light coat off the hook.

> > GLORIA
> > ...awfully good of you. What with the move and the unpacking, we just need a little time to collapse.

> Joss's phone bleeps at her. She pulls it out of her back pocket and silences it with a poke of the thumb, not even looking at it.

> > JOSS
> > I don't blame you. You know moving is the second most stressful thing, after the death of a loved one.

> Her phone bleeps again.

> > WARD
> > Someone is trying to text you.

> Joss takes a brief, irritable glance at the screen.

> > JOSS
> > Someone missed the message I'm working tonight.

> > ROB
> > So Joss: you think your boyfriend—

> The phone bleeps. Joss grimaces.

> > JOSS
> > —Carter.

> > ROB
> > Can Carter stop by and get our router set up? These kids, they turn into little *devils* if they aren't connected.

> > JOSS
> > Carter can handle it. He's with the Dweeb Division at Best Big, he spends all day getting people online.

> > GLORIA
> > All right. Best of luck. We'll be praying for your survival.

Gloria and Rob erupt into laughter.

                    ROB
          Just kidding! We're not religious.

Joss offers a perplexed smile and watches them go out. Her phone bleeps yet again as the door shuts. She doesn't look at it, but Ward tips his head to read the screen.

                    WARD
          Maybe you should just tell him whether you're
          wearing any underwear.

Joss shoots Ward a startled look—then notices Gloria left her purse on an end table.

                    JOSS
          Oops! Your mom left her purse.

She grabs it and opens the door and steps outside.

19   EXT. ROB/GLORIA'S HOUSE—DUSK   19

Joss peers into an empty yard. They're already gone. She frowns, then notices the scarecrows in their rocking chairs... dressed exactly like Rob and Gloria. How unsettling. Joss shakes it off.

              JOSS (calling into the house)
          Should I start dinner?

The door clicks shut.

20   INT. ROB/GLORIA'S HOUSE—KITCHEN—NIGHT   20

Joss yanks a full garbage bag out of the can under the sink, then looks around, not sure what to do with it.

Pam sits at the table, staring through her tablet at a block of knives. A giant kitchen knife protrudes from the cedar block. Pam uses a stylus to doodle on the screen, drawing pink and golden wings on the knife handle.

                    PAM
          The cans are at the end of the drive. Be careful. Ward
          put a Gruesome Garbage Mouth in one of them.

                                        (CONTINUED)

CONTINUED:

JOSS
I had to face one of those the night of the senior
Prom. Chris Golden in his blue tux. Yuck! Thanks for
the warning, but I think I'll live. What'chu doing?

PAM
I'm making a butterfly knife! It's the prettiest. What do
you think?

Joss leans over to look through the screen of Pam's tablet. The wings on
the knife wave slowly.

JOSS
That's pretty sharp!

She winks and slips out, dragging the garbage bag. Pam watches her go.
When Joss is gone, Pam double-taps her screen: **RENDERING.**

The knife sprouts hummingbird-like wings, vibrates right out of the cedar block, and flits away. Pam grins.

> PAM
>
> You bet.

21   EXT. ROB/GLORIA'S HOUSE—NIGHT   21

Joss lugs the garbage down to the road, bins await her.

She doesn't see the gaunt figure in the hoodie, watching her, Michael Myers-like, from down the street. We lose sight of him when she lifts the lid to the first trash can. She wrinkles her nose at the stench. This one is full. She puts the lid back on and our Michael Myers is *right behind her, terrifyingly still.*

She opens the second can: this one is crammed with cardboard boxes. She sighs, shifts her attention to the third can.

The figure in the hoodie leans in from behind her. His tongue reaches out to lick the back of her ear and—

—she wails, drops the bag, and whirls, ready to fight. The dude in the hoodie, CARTER, howls with laughter. Carter is a good-looking orangutan, the Tabasco sauce in the sensible banquet of Joss's life.

> JOSS
>
> Carter! You herpes sore! You should've been here an hour ago.

> CARTER
>
> I texted you I was gonna be late. You never got back to me. Dude, I wish I videoed that. You just about jumped out of your clothes. Which is what I was hoping you'd do later, but now is fine, too. What's got you so wired?

> JOSS
>
> I almost hit someone with my car today. Right on this corner. I was looking at my stupid phone instead of the road and nearly ran over this crazy homeless person. Afterward he screamed a bunch of stuff at me and wandered off. I keep worrying he'll crawl out

(CONTINUED)

CONTINUED:

> from under a rock someplace and freak me out again.
> Also: the kids. They're creepy and depressing. They
> don't do anything. They just sit there looking at their
> tablets. It's like that glowing screen has sucked all the
> life out of them, like—

Carter isn't listening. He's staring at his phone, texting with someone. Joss glares.

JOSS (CONT'D)

> What?

CARTER

> Hm? Your mom wants to know if you're okay 'cause
> you aren't answering your phone. I'm letting her
> know you aren't dead, you just don't love her enough
> to take her calls. What were you saying?

JOSS

> Wasn't important. I'm glad you're here. I need some
> stupid fun to take my mind off the little zombies.

CARTER

> Nice! Wait. Which am I? Stupid or fun?

JOSS

> You're... *multidimensional.* You're like a Swiss Army
> Knife, only instead of a corkscrew, you've got—

CARTER

> A penis. I see where you're going with this.

JOSS

> Oh, good.

He squeezes her and lays on a kiss. Then he grabs the trash, opens the lid on the third can, throws the bag in, closes it. They walk away. HOLD ON THE CAN. HOLD. HOLD.

The lid rattles as *something within* exhales a weary sigh.

CARTER (V.O.)

Dude. Dude. Duuuude.

22   INT. ROB/GLORIA'S HOUSE—KITCHEN—NIGHT   22

CARTER

I mean: **Dude.**

Carter is bent over to look at Ward's tablet. Ward is showing it off, but if he takes any pride in a device that makes the iPad look like a toaster, he doesn't show it.

CARTER (CONT'D)

That's, like, *Star Trek: Into Righteous.* What kind of apps are you running?

(CONTINUED)

CONTINUED:

> WARD
>
> This is the best one. You can draw right on the screen
> and then it tweaks reality to make it come to life. Like:
> look.

He holds the tablet up, and stares through it at some big plate glass
windows. He draws a childish sun on the screen and taps it... and
suddenly the view outside is lit by a bright morning sun.

> WARD (CONT'D)
> Look! Tomorrow morning's sun, today!

He lowers the tablet, and of course the picture windows are still dark
with night. The illusion of daylight can be seen through the screen of the
device only.

Pam and Joss watch from a few paces away.

> JOSS
>
> Pretty cool. Of course, if you want to see tomorrow's
> sun for real, you have to go to bed. Which reminds
> me. C'mon, you guys. Into your jammies, time to
> unplug.

Joss leads Pam out. Carter follows reluctantly. Ward waits until they're
gone... then slyly double-clicks the sun on the screen of his tablet. The
kitchen floods with impossible daylight. Tomorrow's sun today.

23   INT. ROB/GLORIA'S HOUSE—LIVING ROOM—NIGHT   23

An attractive if conventionally decorated space. It could be the living
room in a showroom house. The widescreen TV mounted on the wall is a
glassy blank.

Joss herds the children across the room, in the direction of a back hall and a
bedroom. But halfway there, Carter cranes his neck to look at Pam's tablet.

> CARTER
> What else can you pull up on that thing?

Pam holds up the screen and looks through it at the couch.

> PAM
> I've been throwing Grabby Grabbers around the house.

She pulls a loathsome-looking black hand out of the menu bar and attaches it to the couch. Immediately this rubbery black hand begins to grasp blindly about.

> CARTER
>
> More.

Pam adds a small forest of searching, awful hands.

> CARTER (CONT'D)
> Be careful when you sit down, Joss. You might find
> evil hands wandering all over you.

> JOSS
> Guys, come on—you two—I *said*, let's go—You can
> have this back—

She grabs at Pam's tablet, trying to tug it out of her hand. Pam shrieks as if Joss were yanking her pigtails. Joss lets go in shock.

> JOSS (CONT'D)
> Whoa, whoa! No one is being torn apart here.

> PAM
> It's mine. It's my window. You can't have it.

> JOSS
> Okay. I shouldn't have grabbed it. I just want you to
> give the screen a rest long enough to brush your teeth.
> Now let's go. Ándale!

A rattled Joss steers Ward out of the room. Carter hurries after. Pam remains behind, an ugly look on her face. She double-taps her tablet, then follows them out.

HOLD on the couch. For a long moment nothing happens. Then a horrible, obscene hand of black rubber creeps out from under the cushions and grasps the remote control.

The TV pops on, the sound muted. The picture shows a woman screaming and then a knife coming down and a spray of blood.

BLACK.

(CONTINUED)

CONTINUED:

ACT III

24   INT. ROB/GLORIA'S HOUSE—HALLWAY—NIGHT   24

Joss eases out of a darkened bedroom, pulling the door most of the way shut behind her. Carter stands a few paces off, texting.

> JOSS
>
> Have you ever seen anything like it? It was like I was trying to saw off her hand.
>
> (waits)
>
> Carter?

Carter looks up blankly.

> CARTER
>
> Hm? Totally. Yes. No? What was the proper response to that question? Actually... what was the question?

> JOSS
>
> I hate it. You know? The hold those things have on everyone.

> CARTER
>
> Oh, like you're so much better. Who almost killed a guy today, texting and driving?

> JOSS
>
> I'm not any better! You think it'll be cool to own one of these things, but really they own you. One of these days I'm going to sling my phone through a window and get back my life.

> CARTER
>
> But, baby, if you get rid of your phone, how will I text you pictures of my junk?

> JOSS
>
> Wow! That's so sexy.

CARTER

Master of the turn-on, right here.

JOSS

You know what you can turn on next? The router. I'll leave you to that.

Exunt Joss.

Carter sees a featureless door, reaches for the knob, and

PAM (O.S.)

Don't go in there.

CONTINUED:

Pam peers at him from her half-open bedroom door.

> PAM (CONT'D)
> Ward put the *Bad Thing* in there. The wires and
> electronic stuff is the next door down.
>
> (beat)
>
> Joss shouldn't have tried to take away my window.
> That's not fun. I hate people who aren't fun.

> CARTER
> You kids don't stay in bed, we're going to find out if the
> Bad Thing wants a couple disobedient hors d'oeuvres.

She gives him a tragic look and disappears into her room. He moves on down the hall, finds the closet with the modem in it, and crouches to begin work.

The door he almost opened? The knob rattles gently, then is still.

25   INT. ROB/GLORIA'S HOUSE—LIVING ROOM—NIGHT   25

Joss hesitates next to the couch, frowning at the TV. Who turned that on? She flips it off, then drops on the couch with her Spanish text. She opens it and begins to conjugate the verb for *frightened*.

> JOSS
> Tengo miedo... tienes miedo... tenemos miedo...

Those black rubber hands slide out from under the cushions, blindly grasping for her. She doesn't notice a finger twirling her hair.

Another black hand reaches up between her partly spread legs in a gesture at once both comically obscene and terrifying.

In the kitchen, Joss's phone plays its little jingle. Joss slaps her Spanish text closed and the grabby grabbers immediately leap back into hiding.

> JOSS (CONT'D)
> Carter, that better not be you, texting me when you
> could just walk down the hall!

She stalks swiftly out of the living room and on into...

26   INT. ROB/GLORIA'S HOUSE—KITCHEN—BRIGHTEST DAY   26

Where she takes three steps toward the kitchen table, grabbing her phone... and then freezes, her eyes glazing over. It is, impossibly, early morning outside. She turns her head and looks back into the living room.

27   INT. ROB/GLORIA'S HOUSE—LIVING ROOM—DARKEST NIGHT   27

Joss looks like she just took a swift blow upside the head.

28   INT. ROB/GLORIA'S HOUSE—KITCHEN—BRIGHTEST DAY   28

Joss's legs are shaking. She backs away into...

29   INT. ROB/GLORIA'S HOUSE—LIVING ROOM—NIGHT   29

Retreating to the couch.

> JOSS (wheezes)
> Carter. C-Carter.

She opens her mouth to wail—and then catches herself again, as the butterfly knife buzzes into view, dipping this way and that like a hummingbird on coke. It really is like Tinkerbell reimagined as a murder weapon.

Joss stares back at TINKER-KNIFE, frightened and mesmerized. She backs against the couch. Just as she seems to be gathering the air to scream, one of those black hands catches hold of her ponytail. Another reaches around her waist and together they pull her down onto the couch.

Joss struggles, as half a dozen hands paw at her, and begin pulling her down into the couch, as if there were a bottomless pit under the cushions. One of those hands slithers out and covers her mouth as she's about to shriek. The butterfly knife zips this way and that, appearing to follow the action like a spectator at a tennis match.

Another black hand reaches for the remote control and pops the TV back on, then manipulates the volume, turning it up. On the screen, a new victim screams *at the top of her lungs.*

30   INT. ROB/GLORIA'S HOUSE—HALLWAY—NIGHT   30

Carter pulls himself partway out of the closet at the sound of screaming on the TV.

> CARTER
> Joss?

(CONTINUED)

CONTINUED:

31   INT. ROB/GLORIA'S HOUSE—LIVING ROOM—NIGHT   31

The perverse black rubber hands have pulled Joss deeply into the couch. In another minute she'll be gone.

32   INT. ROB/GLORIA'S HOUSE—HALLWAY—NIGHT   32

Carter scowls, starts down the hall... then catches himself. Remember the door Pam told him not to open? It just jiggled.

> CARTER
> All right. Look, you kids need to be in bed, not
> running around—

He flings open the door. The black tentacles we last saw on the construction site erupt from the open door and fasten themselves to Carter's torso, legs, and throat.

Carter grabs the edges of the door frame and plants his feet to either side of the doorway, before the Bad Thing can yank him into darkness.

33   INT. ROB/GLORIA'S HOUSE—LIVING ROOM—NIGHT   33

Joss is sucked down into the couch—all except one flailing arm. Her free hand lashes blindly about—

—and then seizes the butterfly knife by the handle.

She begins to lay about her with the blade, stabbing the couch cushions, here, there, and everywhere. A blizzard of goose-feathers whirls through the air.

34   INT. ROB/GLORIA'S HOUSE—HALLWAY—NIGHT   34

The tentacles strain like high-tension cables. The edges of the door frame begin to split and pull apart in Carter's powerful grip.

Pam and Ward have emerged from their bedroom to watch.

> CARTER
> Please! Do something!

> PAM
> We are.

> WARD
> We're watching. This is the most fun thing to happen
> since you got here.

Carter looks at them in horrified disbelief.

In the next instant there is an arm across Pam's throat. Joss stands behind her, holding the butterfly knife to one side.

> JOSS
> Stop it, Ward. Or... or I let this knife fly.

Ward gives her an icy look but taps his tablet. The tentacles let go of Carter, drop him hard to the floor. The doorway seems to inhale them. They squirm out of sight and the door slams behind them. Carter clutches his throat, gasping.

Ward continues to tap things on his screen.

ON WARD'S SCREEN:

A pop-up window shows a view of the front porch and the scarecrows. He taps something. **RENDERING.**

> JOSS (CONT'D)
> Put that down.

> PAM
> You put it down! Mother and Father will be angry!
> You are not a very good babysitter!

35   EXT. ROB/GLORIA'S HOUSE—CONTINUOUS   35

The scarecrows sit in the wicker chairs.

36   INT. ROB/GLORIA'S HOUSE—HALLWAY—CONTINUOUS   36

> JOSS
> What the hell is that thing?

> PAM
> It's a kind of window. It's a window to the Darkside.

> JOSS
> Darkside?

37   EXT. ROB/GLORIA'S HOUSE—CONTINUOUS   37

Only now those scarecrows are Rob and Gloria.

(CONTINUED)

CONTINUED:

Rob and Gloria rise and move around the house, entering through an open bay in the garage. Gloria reaches for a shovel. Rob takes up a hand-held blowtorch. Intercut this with the standoff taking place in the hall.

38   INT. ROB/GLORIA'S HOUSE—HALLWAY—CONTINUOUS   38

> WARD
>
> It's not a place. The Darkside is more like a... force. It's like all the daydreams and nightmares ever dreamed, collected together into a big tidal wave. The old world is going to drown.

> PAM
>
> It made us and it made our little windows. It set us free. It's setting lots of things free. Things that used to be make-believe but aren't anymore.

> WARD
>
> We're some of the first. But we won't be the last. It's just getting started.

> CARTER
>
> Christ, Joss, can we skip the Mexican standoff and get out of here?

As he's saying this, the door at the end of the hall—the door into the garage—opens. Rob and Gloria stalk in behind our heroes. Gloria has a shovel. Rob has a hand-held blowtorch, which ignites with a soft WHUMP.

> GLORIA
>
> You can kiss your tip goodbye, young lady.

> ROB
>
> That's for sure.

Carter rolls as Gloria brings the shovel down, taking a chop out of the floor. Then he's up, driving his shoulder into her, throwing her back into Rob. Gloria's blouse ripples with flame.

> ROB (CONT'D)
>
> Oops! Sorry!

Gloria staggers forward, grabbing for Carter. Rob follows, brandishing the blowtorch.

Joss lets go of Pam, shoves her into her brother. She lets go of the butterfly knife, too, and Carter and Joss run. Ward and Pam recover to turn and watch them go.

39   INT. ROB/GLORIA'S HOUSE—FRONT HALL—NIGHT   39

Carter and Joss are sprinting for the front door—our view is theirs—when the butterfly knife zips in from behind and blocks the way, stabbing at them (at us). Its wings hum, making it sound like a giant agitated wasp.

40   INT. ROB/GLORIA'S HOUSE—LIVING ROOM—NIGHT   40

Joss and Carter veer into the living room. Black hands flail from the couch, grasping for them. Joss screams, grabs Carter, yanks him back and away.

41   INT. ROB/GLORIA'S HOUSE—KITCHEN—DAY   41

Carter and Joss retreat, Carter looking around in bewilderment at that impossible sunlight.

(CONTINUED)

CONTINUED:

Ward and Pam appear in the doorway, their "Father" right behind them. In the background, Mom, still burning—she's a walking torch—runs past going one way, then staggers by going the other. No one pays her any mind as she reels back and forth, which is, let's face it, pretty hilarious.

> ROB
> You better believe I won't be writing a
> recommendation letter for you anytime soon, honey.

> WARD
> Shut up, father-thing. You aren't even real.

> ROB
> Oh. All right.

Pam is busy with her screen, tapping it with the stylus. Every knife in the cedar block bursts into the air, wings beating furiously, surrounding our heroes.

> CARTER
> What do we do? Any ideas?

> JOSS
> Smash the window.

> WARD
> No! Don't let them touch it, sister!

> PAM
> Of course I won't. You'll die before I'd let you close
> enough to do anything to my Darkside window. You'll
> both die.

> JOSS
> Not that window.

And she slings her phone through the picture window... that window filled with tomorrow's forgiving daylight. Bright blades of glass spin through the air. Joss and Carter tumble after the phone and into...

42   EXT. ROB AND GLORIA'S HOUSE—RUIN—DAY   42

Joss and Carter spill across the grass. When they sit up, they are holding hands. Their faces are studies in amazement.

The place has become a blackened and smoldering ruin. Only one wall still stands upright, the wall containing the window they just leapt through.

From a high angle we can see a couple fire engines out front. A single fireman sprays down the charred wreck in a desultory sort of way.

43   INT. ROB/GLORIA'S HOUSE—KITCHEN—NIGHT   43

Pam and Ward stare out the window: likewise holding hands. Behind them, the living room is a blazing oven. Our wicked children can see the lovers, but Joss and Carter can't see them. Outside—out in the future day—a dazed Joss picks her phone out of the grass.

Rob stands at dazed attention. Knives hover, waiting for a command.

>   WARD
> They don't see us, do they?

>   PAM
> No. They jumped through the window into tomorrow.
> We're still in tonight. I didn't think they could do that.

>   WARD
> Do what?

>   PAM
> We turned the world upside-down. Then they stood
> on their heads.
> (beat)
> This place is lost. Come on. We'll find someplace else
> where we can have fun.

Pam holds up her tablet and draws a crude door, set into a wall. **RENDERING**.

When she lowers it, there's a door there—a crooked, misshapen door, of the sort a child might draw. She opens it. Beyond is a rainy street somewhere else (China?): neon lights, strange faces.

                                                                (CONTINUED)

CONTINUED:

Ward takes her hand and they step through the door. Pam waves at their strawman father, and pulls the door shut.

Rob waves back—although they're already gone—a forlorn look on his face. The chandelier falls with a shocking crash in the next room.

The house burns, fire consuming curtains, wallpaper, the calendar on the wall. Hold on Rob, looking morose.

DISSOLVE TO:

44   EXT. ROB AND GLORIA'S HOUSE—RUINS—DAY   44

And Rob's charred body of straw. Nothing remains of the house but a debris field of cinders and broken glass.

Joss backs from the wreck, her eyes still astonished. Carter retreats with her, his phone out, filming the smoking, blasted ruin. She looks at him.

                    JOSS
        What are you doing?

                    CARTER
        What do you think? This is going right on YouTube.

She looks at him with dawning horror as he backs away to get a wide view of the house. Her own phone goes off in her pocket. She slips it out, looks at it—then drops it and crunches it under one heel.

Joss approaches THE FIREMAN, who is spraying down the blasted heap, while chewing on a match.

In the background, we see Carter film his dumbass video.

                    JOSS
        Did anyone die?

                    THE FIREMAN
        Mhm? No. No one in the house, thanks be.
        Something like this happens, man, you just can't
        believe it had a happy ending.

Joss backs away from the ruin.

> JOSS

Carter? Did you hear that? They didn't find any
bodies. Do you believe that? Do you—Carter?

She turns in a circle, looking for him. But Carter, man, he's gone, baby,
gone. She does not notice his phone, lying on the blacktop. She drifts
into the road, staring up the street.

> JOSS (CONT'D)

Carter? *CARTER!*

She begins to run—half-hysterical—looking for him.

HOLD ON THAT LINE OF TRASHCANS. Hold. Hold.

The third trashcan burps, rattling the lid.

SLAM CUT TO BLACK

THE SLEEPWALKER

DARKSIDE PILOT—EPISODE 2: "THE SLEEPWALKER"
ACT I

1   EXT. SKY/ZIGGY'S BACKYARD—SUNSET   1

On a SLOW-MO shot of a ripped superhero, naked except for red trunks and red silk cape flowing behind him. ZIGGY ZALIBAN has the body of an Olympic swimmer, the sly smile of a youthful Tom Cruise, and the chiseled chin and golden locks of Buster Crabbe. ZIG has a pair of red Zs—Zz—drawn on his chest in lipstick.

No sound except a faint whoosh of the breeze.

ZIGGY (V.O.)
Ever have one of those dreams where you're flying?

(CONTINUED)

CONTINUED:

Sound rises. The image speeds up. Music roars: "The Girl Got Hot" by Weezer or some other song appropriate to a party hard beer commercial.

Ziggy crashes into a backyard hot tub packed with beach girls in bikinis, inciting screams.

> ZIGGY (V.O.)
> Yeah. I used to have that dream too. Back when I had
> time to sleep.

Ziggy's cannonballs lead into a montage straight out of a Porky's summer movie.

Here is a guy with a FAUXHAWK, in grimy tightie-whities and nothing else, on all fours, with a checkerboard balanced on his back. Ziggy plays checkers with a hot girl in a largely symbolic bikini. They're using shot glasses for pieces. Zig skips one of her pieces and she drinks. Revelers party in the background.

2   INT. ZIGGY'S BATHROOM—NIGHT—INTERCUT   2

And here is Ziggy in a handsome bathroom, sitting on the edge of a tub filled with ice and beers. He makes out with a random cutie, until, in a moment of distraction, they topple over into the Arctic slurry. They shout with laughter, but rather than climb out, they stay there, and keep necking.

3   EXT. ZIGGY'S BACKYARD—NIGHT—INTERCUT   3

Back to the chessboard, where the girl in the bikini hops four of Zig's pieces. He stares in dismay. She smirks.

Jump to later in the evening, as Fauxhawk does his own heroic leap into the hot tub, still wearing his nasty undies. The girls quickly depart in disgust, leaving him confused.

> ZIGGY (V.O.)
> The summer I was nineteen, I didn't need to catch up
> on my dreams. I was *living* them. I had the summer
> place on Brody Island to myself, five days out of seven,
> while my mom was in San Francisco, making
> buttloads of cash as a divorce lawyer to Internet
> zillionaires. I could sleep all morning and stay out all
> night. No rules, no expectations. In between, I had the

dream job at Forever Summer Pools as head lifeguard
to keep me busy. 98% of that job is about one thing:
looking good. And day after day, I rose to the challenge.

4   INT. FOREVER SUMMER POOLS—DAY   4

Long lingering shot of Ziggy standing heroically on his lifeguard tower,
his sculpted muscles gleaming with oil.

Here we are at Forever Summer Pools, a vast indoor Olympic-sized pool
facility, crowded with buff young things. Kids yell and slap the water,
playing a game of basketball in the shallow end. Older folks do laps in
some roped-off lanes.

A girl, fully dressed, nineteen-year-old MADELINE, moves here and
there, taking photos with a nice-looking camera, a bag over one shoulder.

Fauxhawk—now dressed in
swim trunks—snaps a towel at
Ziggy. Ziggy grins, turns, grabs a
towel, and lunges after him.
Fauxhawk dives past Maddy,
who takes a step away to let him
by. Ziggy is right behind him and
brushes Maddy as he goes past.
She spins, off balance, and
crashes into the pool.

Ziggy turns back, remorseful and
surprised. Fauxhawk only waits
around long enough to make
sure Maddy isn't hurt, before
slinking into the background.

Maddy comes up sputtering.

                    MADELINE
Oh you—*you*—steaming pile of stupid!

                    ZIGGY
Sorry, Madeline. Sorry.

He reaches into the pool and helps her out. Her camera is soaked. Water
pours from her shoulder bag.

                                        (CONTINUED)

CONTINUED:

> She sits dripping on the edge, while he drapes her with a towel.

                    ZIGGY (CONT'D)
What are you *doing* here? I thought you hated chlorine
and... children laughing... and fun... and stuff.

                    MADELINE
I'm taking pictures for the website. I need the cash for
school.

> She dumps her bag: out falls a phone and soggy paperbacks.

                    ZIGGY
Your *phone!*

                    MADELINE
My *books.*

                    ZIGGY
Who brings books to a swimming pool?

                    MADELINE
I don't know, people who *like* reading? People who
think books are more entertaining than whipping
people with towels and shoving innocent bystanders
into the pool?

                    ZIGGY
Hey, look. I can fix your phone. Probably the camera
too. Let me have them overnight. All you have to do is
put 'em in a bag of—

                    MADELINE
Do you even vaguely *remember* what it's like to read a
book?

> A squealing sound, like someone pulling a needle across a record. Picture
> freezes.

                    ZIGGY (V.O.)
Of course I remember. She knows I do. I knocked her
down, now it's her turn to do the same to me.

5   INT. CAFE—RAINY DAY   5

Ziggy, younger, less confident, in a hoodie and a pair of glasses, sits with Madeline over cups of coffee. He has a book open, studying the page. She directs his attention to the right lines with one finger.

> ZIGGY (V.O.)
> My senior year I overslept the final in English and got a D on my report card. Bad news: they won't even *look* at your application for lifeguard at Forever Summer unless you made honor role. As if life-guarding has anything to do with grades. But Mr. Mitchell gave me a deal. Madeline was doing a special reading project over winter break—she was filming a scene from *Richard III*, as part of an application for some big-deal Shakespearean study program in England. If I assisted her, *and* she got accepted, he'd give me an A. This was totally ridiculous.
>
> Totally blackmail. I totally said yes.

6   INT. THEATER—NIGHT   6

Madeline and Ziggy, dressed in street clothes, sit on the edge of a stage in front of a dim, empty theater. They each read from a copy of *Richard III*.

> MADELINE
> What was your dream, my lord? I pray you tell me.

> ZIGGY
> Methoughts I dreamt of Jennifer Lawrence making out with Taylor Swift, and oh then it was the season of dear Dick's discontent...

She swats him.

7   INT. ZIGGY'S BASEMENT—NIGHT   7

Madeline and Ziggy read in front of the television, the sound off. Ziggy lounges on the floor, his brow furrowed, intent on the text. Madeline sits above him, on the couch, with her leg draped over his shoulder. Check it out: Ziggy is really into the reading. Maddy notices and smiles a little and—shyly—fusses with his hair. He doesn't notice.

(CONTINUED)

CONTINUED:

8   INT. THEATER—NIGHT   8

Now a video camera records them, as they perform in costume.

MADELINE

What was your dream, my lord? I pray you tell me.

ZIGGY

*Methoughts I had broken from the Tower and was
embarked to cross to Burgundy...*

The picture blurs, softening around the edges.

CLOSE ON A CAMERA LENS, SPECKLED WITH WATER.

9   INT. FOREVER SUMMER POOLS—DAY   9

Zig picks up Maddy's camera and shakes the water off it. He's already got
her phone, wrapped up in a towel.

ZIGGY

I remember you got to go to England and Mr. Mitchell
gave me my A. I remember it worked out great and we
both got what we wanted. Isn't that what you remember?

MADELINE

Yeah. I guess that's what I remember.

But she doesn't mean it and she's hurt.

Ziggy backs away, then pauses, and beams his winning, boyish smile.

ZIGGY

I *wish*—I wish I could still remember my *lines.*

(struggles with his memory)

*As we paced upon the giddy footing of the hatches,
methought my brother stumbled, and in falling struck me
overboard into the tumbling billows of the main...* What
came next?

MADELINE

No idea. I haven't thought about it in ages. I don't
think there's any reason to get hung up on an old
scene. Isn't that exactly your point?

ZIGGY
Yeah. I guess. Hey. Really sorry about—about *this*.

Gesturing helplessly at her water-logged stuff. Maddy wrings out her hair and watches him go.

MADELINE
Oh Lord, methought what pain it was to drown.

Zig yawns into the back of his fist, crossing to the lifeguard tower. He passes an older couple at the edge of the pool. We hold up, pausing to visit with them.

One of them, BO MILLER, sits on the ledge, legs dangling in the water. Bo is fifty, a brawny working man, more comfortable in a hard hat than in that hilarious orange Speedo he's wearing. His wife is down in the water, peering up at him. It's possible to see some scar tissue peeking above her one-piece, a trophy of her triple bypass.

BO
That's it for me. You ready for the sauna?

(CONTINUED)

CONTINUED:

> ELLEN
> Babe, I got another twenty-five laps.

> BO
> Don't you think you oughta take it easy?

> ELLEN
> I am taking it easy. You know how many laps I was
> doing last year this time? I haven't even done half that.
> And don't you lecture me, Bo Miller. Falling asleep in
> front of *General Hospital* doesn't make you a doctor.

Bo leans forward and kisses her. She straightens her swim cap and pushes off the side. He watches her swim away.

Ziggy climbs to his high wooden seat and settles in, putting a pair of mirrored shades over his eyes. He yawns again.

> ZIGGY (V.O.)
> As I was saying. 98% of this job is about looking good.

Ziggy shuts his eyes behind his sunglasses.

> ZIGGY (V.O.) (CONT'D)
> The other 2% is not letting anyone drown.

Ellen does a long slow crawl out to the deep end. There isn't anyone else out there.

Kids yell and splash in the shallows. Teenage girls sit on deck chairs, laughing and talking. One of them turns up the volume on her boom box.

Ziggy slumps down, asleep behind his sunglasses.

Ellen, in the deep end, and largely alone, blinks and blows a hard breath. She turns her head and looks around.

> ELLEN'S P.O.V.:

Lights have halos around them. The pool doesn't seem to have any edges. Sounds have gone hollow and strange.

> BACK TO: Ellen:

Panting hard and clutching her chest.

> ELLEN
> Oh. Oh no.

But who is going to hear her over:

A) Kids splashing, hollering.

B) The girls laughing and their music blasting.

C) A swim instructor in the shallow end blowing a whistle at some tweens who are wrestling.

Ellen opens her mouth to shout for help and swallows water instead, begins to cough. She struggles to the edge of the pool, grabs the side, begins to lift herself out—and slips, bangs her head on the edge of the pool.

> CUT TO:

The kids goofing.

One of the seated girls, laughing as she does her nails.

A gaunt, old fellow breast-strokes his way along one of the lap lanes, then slows at the sight of Ellen Miller... drifting facedown, a little blood trickling from her head. The old man begins to shout in a reedy voice.

> OLD FELLA
> Help! Somebody... help!

10   INT. FOREVER SUMMER POOLS—LIFEGUARD CHAIR—   10
       CONTINUOUS

That shouting voice seems to come from a long way off. Ziggy stirs, half yawns. And then, as the screams rise, he leaps to his feet, eyes popping open wide. The color drains from his face and a stricken look of something that can only be described as horror rises to his features.

> FADE OUT:

ACT II

> FADE IN:

11   EXT. BRODY ISLAND COURTHOUSE—DAY   11

Ziggy descends the courthouse steps, hands shoved in the pockets of his tailored wool slacks, accompanied by his lawyer and his MOTHER. Mom looks good herself, a chrome beauty and a courtroom surgeon in her own right.

> (CONTINUED)

CONTINUED:

Beneath his golden boy tan, Ziggy has the waxy look of an embalmed and badly made-up corpse in his coffin.

ZIGGY (V.O.)

No one knew. No one had any idea I was asleep when she drowned. As far as the world was concerned, I was on duty the whole time. The coroner expressed doubts she could've been saved even with timely action—something about a weakness in the wall of her heart. The hearing was over in an hour. The judge even told me not to blame myself.

Bo Miller is close to the bottom of the steps, in a huddle of middle-aged men and women in cheap off-the-rack suits. He twists his head around, catches sight of Ziggy, and bulls toward him. Some of his friends grab at his shoulders but he tugs free.

BO

Hey, you! Hey. I don't care what they said in there. You had a job to do and you didn't do it.

> ZIGGY

I'm so—so sorry—

> ZIGGY'S LAYWER

That's not an admission of any responsibility. That's
just a general expression of regrets.

> BO

You might as well have not been there at all. You
might as well have been home in bed. You were asleep
on the job and now my wife is dead.

Bo doesn't mean Ziggy was actually asleep on the job—he's using a
euphemism—but Ziggy twitches and pales, and for a moment his eyes
confess.

> ZIGGY

Asleep?!

> ZIGGY'S LAYWER

Step back, sir. I won't have you harassing my client.

> MOM

Come on, Z.

> ZIGGY

Mr. Miller, I know I... let your wife down... but I don't
think I was... It's hard to remember...

> MOM

Shut up, Zig.

Ziggy's escorts—the lawyer and his mother—hustle him on. Zig shoots a
pleading look back at Bo Miller. Bo meets his gaze with bloodshot, grief-
struck eyes... and just a trace of icy speculation.

12   EXT. ZIGGY'S HOUSE—MORNING   12

We survey the desolation of the summer place, now that the fun is over.
Empty shot glasses and spilled gin make a mess of the chessboard. A pair
of grimy tighty-whities float in the hot tub.

13   INT. ZIGGY'S HOUSE—LIVING ROOM—MORNING   13

(CONTINUED)

CONTINUED:

Zig sleeps in front of his TV. A bottle of whiskey, empty, nestles between his legs. He looks corpse-like and pale and needs to shave.

A home movie-quality video plays on the television, the sound down. It's behind-the-scenes footage from Maddy's Shakespeare project. She's laughing, while he prances on the stage in his ridiculous tights and Elizabethan blouse.

> ZIGGY (V.O.)
> The party was over. I don't know if my friends were
> afraid to see me or if I was afraid to see them. I
> couldn't face the pool again, couldn't go into work.
> Most days I stayed at home and slept. I pulled the
> shades and drowned in motionless, dreamless deeps.

The whiskey bottle falls, clatters to the floor. He stirs, rubs his eyes. Ziggy rises and paces toward the front door. A lawnmower grinds somewhere nearby.

14   EXT. ZIGGY'S FRONT YARD/STREET—DAY   14

Ziggy makes his way down along the walk, to check the mail. Across the street, a wiry old guy drives his riding mower over the green expanse of his lawn. A pair of young moms speedwalk while pushing their strollers. An older fellow with a Hitchcockian build walks a Yorkshire Terrier.

Thunder grumbles from a clear blue sky. An unnatural breeze rises. The streetlights blink on with a dismal drone, brighten, fade. The cars parked along the street come partly to life, headlights and blinker-lights flashing. This is real *Close Encounters* stuff.

Ziggy shades his eyes with one hand, peering around—as the Darkside Event strikes. Everything in the world becomes a negative image of itself, except for Ziggy... and Newman, phasing into existence across the street. The two of them stare at each other in bewilderment. The rest of the world got stuck in place, as if time itself somehow hangs.

> ZIGGY
> What's happening?

> NEWMAN
> Darkside Event! You're right at the center of it.

ZIGGY

What's wrong with everything? No one's moving!

NEWMAN

It'll pass. Quick: think hard. Have you recently done
anything really, really bad or really, really good?

Ziggy gapes.

ZIGGY

Well, I haven't done anything... really, really good.

NEWMAN

That's unfortunate.

The world gives one last great white throb and then the event is over. The
lawn mower rumbles forward. The speedwalkers speedwalk on. No one
seems aware that anything at all has changed.

Newman points a finger at Ziggy.

NEWMAN

Stay where you are. I usually don't have much time,
but I'll try and help before—

Newman yawns. His eyes flutter. His head drifts downward so his chin
rests on his chest. He raises one hand, waving it in a dismissive gesture:
it's cool, don't worry. But then he sinks to one knee and folds over onto
his face.

Ziggy sweeps his gaze around in alarm. The quick-stepping housewives
swerve into each other, knocking heads and going down in a tangle...
asleep before they hit the ground. Their strollers roll down the sidewalk
without them.

The older man—the one who resembled Hitchcock—yawns, sits down in
the grass, lies back, and falls asleep. His dog curls up on his chest and
goes to sleep with him.

The man driving the riding mower falls asleep at the wheel. The mower
veers, running straight at Newman's crumpled body.

Ziggy takes a startled step forward, lifting his arms to cry out, but he's too
late. The riding mower goes over Newman with a dreadful, gristly thud.

(CONTINUED)

CONTINUED:

There's a flash of silvery light, like a flashbulb popping, and Newman is gone.

Ziggy gapes at the street in bewilderment. A kid sails by on a bicycle, abruptly falls asleep, and wipes out: SPLAT! The front tire of his overturned bike spins gaily in the air.

Zig runs to one of the housewives, pulls her arm. She doesn't stir. He tugs at the other.

> ZIGGY
>
> Ma'am? **Ma'am??**

> HOUSEWIFE
>
> No, mommy, it *isn't* a school day.

She rolls away, frowning fretfully, still asleep.

Zig looks around as the riding mower crashes through a line of trash cans and trundles off up the street.

> ZIGGY
>
> What is this? Wake up. One of you—someone—
> *Wake up!*

He grabs the dog and hoists it into the air by its back legs. It sleeps on.

He flips it aside (everyone will laugh except for PETA) and after a moment of indecision runs for his house.

15   INT. ZIGGY'S HOUSE—LIVING ROOM—DAY   15

Ziggy snatches his cell phone off the coffee table and dials 911.

We jump to a split-screen, Ziggy on the left half of the screen and

INTERCUT WITH:

16   INT. EMERGENCY CALL CENTER—DAY   16

On our right. An efficient young woman takes his call.

> ZIGGY
>
> Hello?

> RESPONDER
>
> You've reached 911, what is your—

She pauses, yawns hugely—and then crashes face first onto her desk.

> ZIGGY

Hello? Hello?

Split screen ends as Ziggy hangs up.

He dials a different number. Split-screen again. On the right half of the screen:

INTERCUT WITH:

17   INT. MEETING ROOM—DAY   17

Ziggy's mom is just leaving a conference room with a few businessmen.

> ZIGGY

Ohmigod, mom, something awful is happening.

> MOM

Oh Zigggfffzzffnggg.

She collapses, drool running from the corner of her mouth. Businessmen stare down at her in bewilderment.

> ZIGGY

Mom? **MOM!**

The split screen ends, leaving us alone with Ziggy. Ziggy stares at his phone in horror. His pacing has taken him to a picture window with a view of the yard. He parts the blinds slightly to see what's happening outside.

THROUGH THE WINDOW:

People are up and staggering about, half-awake. One of the speedwalkers has moved to comfort the boy who dumped his bike. The other

(CONTINUED)

CONTINUED:

speedwalker runs to collect the strollers. Hitchcock sits up, holding his little dog in his lap.

18   EXT. ZIGGY'S HOUSE—FRONT YARD—DAY   18

Ziggy bursts through the door.

> ZIGGY
> You're awake!

And they all collapse again. Hitchcock flops back into the grass. His dog curls up comfortably on the slope of his chest. The riding mower buzzes back through the shot, the sleeping driver steering it back the way he came.

Ziggy stands there, pole-axed with wonder and shock.

FADE OUT:

ACT III

FADE IN:

19   INT. CAFE—DAY   19

A pretty young gal admires a bagel slathered in cream cheese... then shuts her eyes and falls face first into it, her wide mouth fixed in a dreamy smile. Splat!

Ziggy wanders through a cafe where everyone is asleep. Coffee cups have been knocked over, and coffee spills across tables to either side of him, dribbling onto the floor, puddling at his feet.

> ZIGGY (V.O.)
> No one could keep their eyes open around me. I put
> people to sleep faster than a *Murder, She Wrote*
> marathon.

20   INT. SUPERMARKET—DAY   20

Zig walks down an aisle in a suburban supermarket. Behind him we can see three or four people asleep on the floor, their carts standing forgotten. He pauses to pick a bag of white rice off the shelf, stares at it with interest.

21   INT. BANK VAULT—DAY   21

Ziggy stands in an open bank vault. Before him are the bags of cash. Behind him, in the foreground, a bank guard sleeps with his thumb in his mouth.

> ZIGGY (V.O.)
> I could've robbed more banks than John Dillinger. No
> one could've stopped me. No one could even watch
> the surveillance footage without falling asleep.

22   INT. SECURITY ROOM—DAY   22

Two Feds in ties and suspenders are asleep in front of a security monitor.
One of them dozes with his head on the other guy's shoulder, his hand
lightly twirling his partner's hair.

ON THE SCREEN: Ziggy stares up into the security camera, his face
filling the screen, his eyes enormous and bewildered.

23   INT. ZIGGY'S HOUSE—LIVING ROOM—DAY   23

And we're close on a giant plastic bag full of rice. Maddy's camera and
phone are both stuck inside. Ziggy opens the bag, slips out the camera.
He presses the power switch and the screen on the back blinks on.

(CONTINUED)

CONTINUED:

ON THE CAMERA SCREEN:

Ziggy cycles through pictures of kids horsing around in the pool...
and slows, as he comes across some pictures Maddy surreptitiously took
of him. Good pictures of a handsome, basically decent young man.

Zig sets aside the camera and digs out the phone, dusts the rice off it.

> ZIGGY (V.O.)
> I kept hoping they'd wake up... or I would. That'd I'd
> snap out of the bad dream I was in and be a human
> being again... instead of a walking sleeping pill.

24   INT. BATTERED OLD CAR—DAY   24

Close on Bo Miller's hand, which holds a bottle of sleeping pills: **DOZ-4-U
SLEEPING PILLS * ZOPICLONE. WARNING: OVERDOSE MAY
CAUSE DEATH! USE AS PRESCRIBED.**

A sunny Beach Boys riff plays on the crappy radio in his crappy sedan. Bo
sits in the parking lot of a liquor store, with a photo album open to a
picture of Ellen and Bo at their fortieth anniversary, cutting a
cake. Bo weeps helplessly.

> BO
> I'll see you soon, baby.

> He shakes a fistful of pills into his
> palm and throws them into his
> mouth. He reaches for a bottle in a
> brown paper bag.

> An ad comes on the radio, a pair
> of sneering young voices, trading
> phrases. The sound of them
> freezes Bo in place.

> FEMALE RADIO VOICE
> It's time to get
> some:

                    MALE RADIO VOICE
Fun!

                    FEMALE RADIO VOICE
Get some:

                    MALE RADIO VOICE
Exercise!

                    FEMALE RADIO VOICE
Get some:

                    MALE RADIO VOICE
Ass...tonishing savings at the Forever Summer Water
Center, where it's never been cheaper to get some of
the best swimming, best diving, and prettiest honeys
on the north coast!

                    FEMALE RADIO VOICE
...and don't forget the rock-hard boys, ladies!

                    MALE RADIO VOICE
It's time to get some!

                    FEMALE RADIO VOICE
And live the dream in a place where it's Forever
Summer...

                    MALE RADIO VOICE
—Forever Summer—

                    FEMALE RADIO VOICE
Forever Summer Water Center. Come on down and
start living the life.

Bo spits out the entire half-melted gob of tablets, and screws the top back
on the bottle. He reaches for the glove compartment and pops it open. He
throws the sleeping pills in—and pulls out a Ruger .44, big enough to
give Dirty Harry a boner.

                         BO
I just got one thing to do first.

                                        (CONTINUED)

CONTINUED:

He slams the glove compartment.

25   EXT. MADELINE'S HOUSE—DAY   25

Maddy comes out the front door of a small, suburban house, her bag over her shoulder, then hitches up, looks at her feet. Her camera sits on the top step, next to a big envelope.

She picks the camera up and turns it on. She smiles sadly.

She wasn't expecting it to work. She tears open the envelope and her phone slides out. She's peering down at it when a message appears on the screen.

TEXT—**ZIGGY: CAN YOU COME TO MY HOUSE? I NEED HELP.**

Maddy frowns.

26   EXT. ZIGGY'S HOUSE—FRONT YARD—DAY   26

Maddy, still dressed for the beach, approaches the front door. She peers uncertainly at the windows: every blind pulled, every shade drawn.

She knocks. A moment passes... and then her phone burbles pleasantly. She slips it out, has a look at a text message. We see what she sees, the text bubble floating on the screen (take a look at the way Josh Boone handled text messages in *THE FAULT IN OUR STARS*—we want it to look like that).

TEXT: **I'm here. Right on the other side of the door.**

Maddy looks away from her phone.

                              MADELINE
          If you're right on the other side of the door, then why
          don't you open it so we can talk like normal people?

TEXT: **I can't let you see me or hear my voice. Something really bad is happening to me.**

                         MADELINE (CONT'D)
          Oh, for chrissake, Ziggy sometimes I get so sick of
          your stupid—

TEXT: **PLEASE! Give me one chance.**

TEXT: **Face the street & DON'T LOOK BACK, even when I open the door. TRUST ME.**

Madeline reluctantly turns around and stares at the street.

MADDY'S P.O.V.:

An old lady collects bags of groceries from the trunk of her car. A housewife waters her flowerbed. A postman sticks envelopes in a mailbox.

The door opens behind Madeline and Ziggy steps into the doorway. She starts to turn, but he puts his hand on her shoulder, keeping her from facing him.

MADDY'S P.O.V.:

The old lady hangs half out of her trunk, legs in the air. The housewife has collapsed into her begonias; the hose squirts pointlessly in the air.

The postman lies in the street, arm stretched over his head, one hand still caught in the mailbox. Maddy's eyes grow enormous. Ziggy retreats into the house. The door bangs shut.

MADDY'S P.O.V.:

The housewife struggles up from behind her peonies. The old lady kicks her legs feebly in the air. The postman lifts his face from the blacktop.

Maddy spins and presses herself to the door.

                    MADELINE (CONT'D)
        What just happened?

                                        (CONTINUED)

CONTINUED:

The mail-slot opens and a notebook falls out: flump.

She slides down the door and sits with her back against it, and the notebook on her knees. The title reads: **I AM THE SLEEPWALKER.**

27   EXT. THE BUSHES—CONTINUOUS   27

Bo Miller watches from the hedge, gun across his knee.

                                                    DISSOLVE TO:

28   EXT. ZIGGY'S HOUSE—FRONT YARD—DUSK   28

Maddy closes the notebook and looks up into the plummy evening, while crickets make soft music. She looks very pretty, and very sad.

> MADELINE
>
> I believe you, you know. All of it.
>
> (pause)
>
> Except maybe the part about it being your fault that woman drowned. She had a weak heart.

TEXT: **IF YOU BELIEVE *ANY* OF IT, BELIEVE THAT PART. I WAS ASLEEP.**

> MADELINE (CONT'D)
>
> And you think somehow that's why this is happening? That you were selected for cosmic justice by this weird— electrical storm or whatever? This Darkside event?

No reply.

Maddy turns, presses one hand against the door, closes her eyes.

> MADELINE (CONT'D)
>
> So what do we do? Do you want me to—bring you a doctor? Or... carry the story to the press?

TEXT: **I WANT YOU TO HELP ME CONFESS. IF I TELL THE TRUTH MAYBE IT WILL STOP.**

> MADELINE (CONT'D)
>
> Good. Good, Ziggy. You could've asked me for anything and I would've done it for you. But I'm glad you asked me to do the right thing.

(pause)

I wish I could hear your voice.

The letterflap opens. Ziggy's lips appear in the slot.

                    ZIGGY
I wish you could too.

Maddy closes her eyes, rests her head against the door. She's already asleep.

                    ZIGGY (CONT'D)
Sometimes I feel like I've been sleepwalking through
my whole life. The only time I was ever really awake
was when I had to help this cute little dork with her
Shakespeare project. I didn't sleep through that. God, I
wish I had spent a little more time with my eyes open.

His finger reaches through the flap and lightly caresses her cheekbone. Then the flap swats shut.

She stirs, opens her eyes, yawns.

                    MADELINE
Unh. I—hey. Did you just try talking to me? Sorry... I
didn't get any of it.

(pause)

So. What now?

TEXT: **NOW YOU DRIVE ME TO THE POLICE.**

TEXT: **THAT NOTEBOOK IS MY CONFESSION. I'M GOING TO TURN MYSELF IN WITH IT.**

                    MADELINE (CONT'D)
How are you going to turn yourself in if everyone falls
asleep as soon as they look at you?

The door opens.

Ziggy stands in it—covered by a heavy wool blanket. Maddy stares up at him for one moment of quiet amazement... but remains awake. She can't see him or hear him, so for the moment, she's safe.

                                        (CONTINUED)

CONTINUED:

29   EXT. ZIGGY'S HOUSE—DRIVEWAY—CONTINUOUS   29

Maddy guides Zig across the yard to his hot little ride. She opens the passenger door and settles Ziggy in his seat, even buckling him up. She shuts the door and starts around the front of the car.

That's when Bo makes his move. He surges from the brush and clouts Madeline in the back of the head. Her legs give. He catches her around the waist before she can fall to the blacktop. She drops the notebook and the car keys.

She isn't quite unconscious but when she moans he shuts her up.

                         BO
          Be quiet if you want to live.

He opens the door to the backseat and shoves her in. She's half limp and doesn't put up a struggle when he points the gun in her face and lifts a finger to his lips: sh. He uses a zip tie to cuff her wrist to the strap above the door, cinching it tight.

He picks the keys out of the driveway, leaves the notebook, and gets behind the wheel. Flicks the headlights on and coasts into the night.

30   EXT. ZIGGY'S CAR—NIGHT   30

No surprise here: Ziggy owns a sleek, show-off ride, something right out of *The Fast & The Furious*. Bo steers them away from town, up into arid hills, among the saguaro and the sage.

31   INT. ZIGGY'S CAR—CONTINUOUS   31

Bo is steering now—in more ways than one.

                         BO
          Hey, Zig. What'chu doing under there?

Ziggy stiffens. Until now, he assumed Maddy was driving.

                      MADELINE
          He's got a gun, Ziggy. He was waiting for us.

                         BO
          I've been waiting all day. What's this little game the
          two of you been playing? What's with the blanket?

(pause)

Come on. Say something. Or are you asleep under there?

                    MADELINE
He can't talk.

                      BO
Why not?

                    MADELINE
You wouldn't—you wouldn't believe me.

32   EXT. ZIGGY'S CAR—NIGHT   32

And Ziggy's racer climbs higher into the hills, accelerating all the time. It's going dangerously fast.

33   INT. ZIGGY'S CAR—NIGHT   33

Bo can't decide whether to smirk or rage and is doing a bit of both.

                      BO
So take off the blanket, I want to see your face.

                    MADELINE
He can't do that, either. Don't do it, Ziggy. We're going too fast.

                      BO
Why can't he? Scared to look me in the eye? Scared to face up to what he took from me? *MY WHOLE LIFE IS GONE.*

                    MADELINE
He's not scared. We were going to the police. He wrote a *confession*. He admits he screwed up. It was all in the notebook. I could've showed you, but you bashed me over the head. If you take us back—

                      BO
(laughs)
Nice try. Points for creativity.

                                        (CONTINUED)

CONTINUED:

>   (pause)
>
>   You know what's funny, Ziggy? I came *thi-i-is* close to
>   doing myself. Sleeping pills.

He takes them out of his pocket, rattles the bottle of tablets, and throws them on the seat, by Ziggy.

>   BO (CONT'D)
>   Then I thought, *oh man, you got this all wrong.* Ziggy is
>   the one needs to catch up on his beauty sleep. Good-
>   looking young man like that can't catch enough Zs.
>   So. You take them. You go on and *get some*, and I
>   won't shoot your girlfriend.

Ziggy hesitates—then nods. The blanket shifts and the pills disappear under the hem.

>   BO (CONT'D)
>   No. Come on. What d'you think, I'm stupid? I hafta
>   *see* you take them. Get that blanket off.

>   MADELINE
>   He can't—

>   BO
>   You shut up, bitch. I'll kill both of you.
>   (to Ziggy)
>   I want to see your face while you swallow them. I
>   want to look at you while you pass out and die. The
>   blanket comes off. *Now.*

Ziggy shakes his head but Bo won't have it.

>   BO (CONT'D)
>   Enough of this crap—

He grabs the blanket. A brief struggle follows, but Bo has the arms of a silverback gorilla and a hundred pounds on Ziggy. The blanket flies free.

Bo's eyes widen—then sag. He collapses across the wheel. In the backseat, Madeline quickly looks away from Ziggy before she can be affected.

P.O.V. THROUGH THE WINDSHIELD:

As Zig's sporty little coupe swerves violently, and at high speed, across the road, with a painful shriek of tires coming apart. There's a flash and everything freezes. The image is overwhelmed by a nearly blinding whiteness.

> ZIGGY (V.O.)
> I don't remember punching through the guardrail. I don't remember flying off the road, leaving the ground.
>
> (beat)
>
> Hey. Ever have one of those dreams where you're flying?

Sounds rise around us: crackling flame. That fierce brightness dims, fades, becomes:

34   EXT. ZIGGY'S CAR—NIGHT   34

Zig's car is upside down, oily black smoke pouring out of it.

35   INT. ZIGGY'S CAR—CONTINUOUS   35

Ziggy stirs, looks around, his confusion changing to fright. He struggles free from his seat belt.

(CONTINUED)

CONTINUED:

He's relatively uninjured, just a little blood trickling from the corner of his bashed mouth. Bo Miller is out, face sunk deep in the air bag. Both eyes are black, swollen shut.

Ziggy looks into the backseat. Madeline's eyes are still closed, face averted.

>   MADELINE
>   I'm all right. Get him out of the car.

36   EXT. ZIGGY'S CAR—CONTINUOUS   36

Ziggy is able to kick his way out through the passenger side window. He runs to the other side of the car. The driver's side window is already gone. Ziggy drags Bo free and sets him down halfway up the hill.

By now, the car is burning pretty good. Ziggy shoots a look toward the top of the hill and the road above. Headlights shush by. He takes one step in that direction—then catches himself.

>   ZIGGY (V.O.)
>   Even then, with all I knew, my first instinct was to run
>   and get help. To wave down another car. But the first
>   person to see me in their headlights would fall asleep
>   and fly off the road themselves. Maybe it would be a
>   minivan with kids in the back. Maybe it would be a
>   schoolbus.

He slides back down the hill, dust and rocks tumbling ahead of him. He reaches Madeline. Her door won't open, but he is able to slide in through the shattered window to be next to her in the whirling smoke and flickering orange light.

She coughs, her face filthy, bloodied, her eyes squeezed shut. Her wrist is still cuffed to the strap.

>   MADELINE
>   I can't. I'm stuck. Ziggy, get out of here.

He fights with the cuff, trying to free her wrist. Bites at it, pulls at it. It would require a pair of lock cutters to snap them. They're both coughing now. As the first flames begin to flicker around them, Ziggy's panic grows... while Madeline becomes ever more calm.

MADELINE (CONT'D)

Ziggy. *Ziggy.* It's all right. You can't help me. You can't get
me out and we both know this car is going up in flames.

He touches her face with the back of his hand, weeping helplessly.

MADELINE (CONT'D)

You want to do something for me? You can send me
off with a good dream, so I don't have to feel any pain.
Will you do that?

She tentatively opens her eyes and smiles at him.

MADELINE (CONT'D)

Will you do that one thing for me, dreamboat?

Her gaze searches his desperate, handsome face. He lightly cups her neck
in his hands, staring back.

MADELINE (CONT'D)

My soul is heavy. I fain would sleep.

ZIGGY

God give Your Grace good rest.

She shuts her eyes, sagging into slumber, her face nestling into the space
between his neck and shoulder. He smooths a hand over her hair,
shivering with misery. Then he lifts his head. He peers into the front seat,
reaches up there, and grasps the bottle of sleeping pills.

The smoke glows the color of hot coals as he tosses back one handful,
then another. He shuts his eyes and clings to his beloved. Of course he
isn't going to leave her. She might wake up before it's over.

We move slowly in on his almost too-handsome face.

ZIGGY (V.O.)

Sleep, perchance to dream. Something like that, right?

(laughs)

I'm not proud of sleepwalking through my life. I'm
not proud of the people I hurt or the lives I destroyed.
But I like to think I was awake at the end. For a
moment, anyway, I had my eyes open.

(CONTINUED)

CONTINUED:

Suddenly he opens his eyes, and fixes US with a piercing blue stare.

ZIGGY

What about you?

DRAW BACK:

37   TO REVEAL THE BLACK BOX.   37

Ziggy's face is just an image on one side of our ever-turning cube of nightmares. The sides of the box continue revolving to show: a man with a bat climbing out of his mouth (see "Black Box"), an older man screaming as a silver ball rolls over him (see "Black Box"), a hideous troll glaring at us (again, from "Black Box").

NEWMAN (V.O.)

I like to think maybe there at the end, there was a little rest for Ziggy, you know? We can hope. That's all I got for you tonight, doc. I gotta close my eyes for a while. I'd tell you I have to turn out the light and get some Z's... but it's always dark here.

(yawns)

Sleep well, doc. Maybe don't look under the bed tonight. Who knows what you might find?

A click. A dial tone. The box revolves around to show a face of perfect, absolute darkness.

END CREDITS.

BLACK BOX

DARKSIDE PILOT—EPISODE 3: "BLACK BOX"

ACT I

FADE IN:

OPEN.

1   INT. FAMILY DEN—LATE AFTERNOON   1

BRIAN NEWMAN, a boy of nine, but serious beyond his years, fiddles with a Rubik's Cube at one end of a cluttered table. Other boys crowd close around. A noisy game of Monopoly is underway.

A TV plays on, unattended, in the background. This is an old TV, with a faux wooden cabinet, and brass antennas. And look what's on: *Tales From the Darkside!* Tonight's episode is my personal favorite: "Word Processor of the Gods."

TITLE: 30 YEARS AGO.

(CONTINUED)

CONTINUED:

NEWMAN has the Cube just about worked out when someone slaps it from his hands.

                    DONNIE
          Wake up, dipstick.

                    GERARD
          Yeah, Brian, it's your turn, are you gonna roll or what?

                    DONNIE
          Let's get this crap over with. Whatever you roll, you're
          gonna land on one of my hotels, and I'm finally going
          to clean your candy ass out.

DONNIE is almost twice Newman's age, and has the strong jaw and handsomely tousled hair of a child model... or a Hitler Youth. GERARD is probably Newman's friend—they're about the same age, and have the same soft, vulnerable look about them. SUSANNAH, Donnie's sister, and her friend LAUREN round out the crowd.

                    GERARD
          Nu-uh, not if he lands on Free Parking. There's so
          much money in there. I bet there's a thousand friggin
          big ones.

                    DONNIE
          Shut up. Your mother has sat on a thousand friggin
          big ones. He'd have to roll snake eyes and it's not
          happening.

          In this world, you're either doomed or a lucky prick.
          You don't get to be both. And anyone who looks at
          Newman's face can see he ain't lucky.

Newman, who still hasn't said a thing, reaches for the dice. His features are fatigued and bloodless, a child coming to the end of a long sickness. But he isn't coming to the end of a sickness—he's just at the start of one that will hold him in thrall for years to come.

But before he can toss the dice, Donnie smacks his hands, and they tumble to the floor.

DONNIE (CONT'D)

Don't get lucky, Newman. If you get lucky... that would
be really *bad* luck. If you understand me. We've been
playing for five hours and I didn't sit here with you
little dimwits for all that time just to lose.

Newman doesn't nod or reply or react at all. Just stares at Donnie somberly
a moment longer, then climbs under the table to collect the dice—

—and comes face to face with a hideous and impossible child. In his shock,
Newman recoils, clouting his head against the underside of the table.

DONNIE (CONT'D)

Dude, what are you doing under there? Stop reaching
for my zipper!

The other players erupt into cruel laughter—even Gerard—but Newman
hardly seems to hear them. He's staring at the thing he just discovered
hiding under
the table.

BIG WINNER
looks almost
exactly like a
photo negative
of Newman
himself. His
skin is cinder-
colored and his
eyes are hot
points of white
light. But
Newman is
casually

dressed, while Big Winner opts for formal attire. His suit is the color of
radioactive ash. His skinny tie is a stripe of midnight.

Newman opens his mouth to scream. Big Winner touches a finger to
smiling lips: *sh.*

His infernally glowing hand passes Newman the dice.

(CONTINUED)

CONTINUED:

>   BIG WINNER
>   (whisper)
>   I fixed them for you.

When he speaks, Big Winner's image flickers and rolls, just like an image on a TV with bad reception.

Newman squats there, shivering.

>   BIG WINNER (CONT'D)
>   Go on. Go play. We're going to be the big winners
>   today, Brian.

Newman scurries away, climbs back up into his chair. He sits at the end of the table, stricken with terror. He has the dice in his hand, but has forgotten all about them. He steels himself, and peeks down below once more—

—but Big Winner is gone.

>   DONNIE
>   Jesus, you're fondling those dice like your momma
>   holding your daddy's balls. *Roll 'em.*

Newman lets them tumble from his hand. Snake eyes.

A cry of jubilation rises from the other children. But it isn't long-lived. Donnie snatches up the dice and turns them over. 1's appear on every side. It's 1's all around.

>   DONNIE (CONT'D)
>   What's this? You think you're funny, you little crapstain?
>   I oughta make you eat your free parking money—

But as Donnie yanks Newman out of his seat, the little boy's eyes roll back in his head. Newman convulses, spittle flying. Donnie, who is, after all, just a kid, responds with instant terror as Newman hits the floor, kicking his heels on the tiles.

>   DONNIE (CONT'D)
>   What the hell! I didn't do nothing to him! Ohmigod.

The other kids close in around him, the whole crowd of them in a state of high distress, especially eleven-year-old Susannah, who was babysitting Brian and Gerard.

SUSANNAH

Mom! Mom, something's wrong with Brian Newman,
come quick!

Brian's seizure continues but we begin to glide away. We've seen enough
here. We leave the children and draw up to the Rubik's Cube, which has
come to rest a few feet away, in front of the TV. Only something has
happened to the cube... it has turned *entirely black on all six sides.*

In the background, the old *Tales From the Darkside* intro rolls on the TV.

OLD INTRO

Man lives in the sunlit world of what he believes to be
reality. But there is—unseen by most!—an underworld
that is just as real... but not so brightly lit! A Darkside!

Hold on this for a single moment and then

SLAM CUT TO:

CREDITS.

Theme music is a lone man whistling the
Darkside theme. Our melody
accompanies a selection of images right
out of your worst fever dreams:

A) a doll rots like a time lapse reel of fruit
going bad.

B) A trollish, blind child stacks a wall of
blocks that reads DIES DARK. He
rearranges them to read DARKSIDE.

C) A crow lands on a street sign at the
corner of BRADBURY and ROMERO. It
flicks an impossible forked tongue at us.

ACT II

2   INT. NEWMAN'S RIDE—DAY   2

TITLE: NOW

Brian Newman sits behind the steering wheel of his battered and rusting
Nissan Cube (ha! Get it? *Get it??* Nevermind...), tearing open envelopes.

(CONTINUED)

CONTINUED:

Now in his mid-thirties, Newman has the wasted look of a heroin junkie coming to the end of his string. His hands shake badly as he goes through his mail, all of it bills. In flashes we see a medical bill for a CAT scan: OVERDUE it reads, next to a large number. The rent is overdue. He's months over on his car payments. The pharmacy wants the co-pay on half a dozen drugs.

Newman digs a bottle of aspirin out of the deep pocket of a coat that looks like it came from the Army-Navy store. Pills spill out, some into his palm, some onto the floor. He dry swallows about six before getting out of the car.

3   EXT. GAME ON—DAY   3

The scene is a dismal strip mall. Newman aims himself at a little hobby shop, GAME ON, specializing in puzzles and board games.

4   INT. GAME ON—CONTINUOUS   4

The interior is dim and cluttered. Stacks of games partially obscure windows that are so dusty they hardly let in any daylight. The buzzing fluorescents aren't doing much for Newman's wan complexion.

He lets himself behind the counter and dings open the cash register, but before he gets any further in setting up for the day, an old man appears from the back of the store.

ABRAMS, Game On's joyless owner, gives Newman a hooded glance and gestures for him to come.

                         MR. ABRAMS
          Newman. My office.

Newman glances at the clock, but it's five-to-five. He's not late.

                         NEWMAN
          Mr. Abrams?

A beaded curtain rattles in a dim doorway. Abrams is already gone.

5   INT. ABRAMS' SEEDY OFFICE—CONTINUOUS   5

Newman lets himself into an office about the size of a large broom closet. Abrams sits behind his desk, playing a game of *Labyrinth*. You know *Labyrinth*? It's a wooden maze. The player guides a ball bearing through it, by tilting the board this way and that. And no, this is not an extraneous detail. It will matter a great deal, later on.

NEWMAN
Everything all right? I should get the new deliveries
scanned into inventory.

ABRAMS
I have a check for you. Under the Rubik's Cube.

Newman picks up the Cube and the envelope beneath it.

NEWMAN
Ah, I already picked up my check for last week.
Thank you, Mr. Abrams.

ABRAMS
It's not for last week. It's for the next two weeks.
You're done. I'll cover tonight's shift.

NEWMAN
You can't fire me because I had a seizure. That's
workplace discrimination.

Mr. Abrams doesn't look at him. His voice is disinterested, his entire focus
on his game.

(CONTINUED)

CONTINUED:

> ABRAMS
>
> I'm not firing you because you had a seizure. I'm firing you for what happened before the seizure.

> NEWMAN
>
> To Mrs. McCartney? Are you saying that's my fault?

Abrams loses a ball into a hole, and snarls, and looks up.

> ABRAMS
>
> You gonna say it wasn't? You going to look me in the eye and say you had nothing to do with it? I knew you had a reputation when I hired you—

> NEWMAN
>
> —I have a reputation?

> ABRAMS
>
> Yeah, you do. You're like the human Bermuda Triangle. I was kind of curious, actually, to see if there was any truth in it. To the stories. Well, my curiosity has been satisfied, and I'm letting you go before you kill the cat. Or one of the customers.

> NEWMAN
>
> She's fine!

> ABRAMS
>
> She's suing. Thank God no one believes her. If she actually gets her case to court, I think the judge would be more likely to order psychiatric treatment than to award her damages.

> NEWMAN
>
> Mr. Abrams... if you could let me continue to work here until I find something different. I would really appreciate it. I won't be any trouble.

> ABRAMS
>
> Don't make promises you can't keep.

NEWMAN
I don't think you understand how important it is to
me, to keep working. To at least have that.

ABRAMS
I understand. I just don't care. You want a job, get
yourself a reality show or something. They love pasty
freaks like you on TV.
(laughs to himself)
Reality television... more like *unreality* television.

He plops a ball bearing into the *Labyrinth* and begins to tilt the board this
way and that.

NEWMAN
Have fun playing with your balls, Mr. Abrams.

Newman brushes out through the beaded curtain. The ball falls through
another hole. Abrams tosses the board aside in irritation, then looks up.

ABRAMS
Hey! I want that Rubik's Cube back! Newman!

6   EXT. GAME ON—DAY   6

Newman reels across the parking lot, absent-mindedly giving his stolen
Rubik's Cube a few turns before tossing it in the air, catching it, putting it
back in his pocket. He jumps in his car.

The engine makes a horrendous grinding noise. It won't start. It's just
been that kind of day, right?

He pops the hood and gets out from behind the wheel and makes his way
around to see if he can spot what's wrong. A little blue smoke trickles up
from the inner works.

He glares down at cables and cylinders. A slender man in a tailored gray
suit joins him at the front fender, a guy about Newman's age, with
intelligent, clever eyes and a wry smile.

FINNEY
Sounds like the catalytic convertor. That's trouble you don't
need. Especially on top of your medical bills, Mr. Newman.

(CONTINUED)

CONTINUED:

Newman sighs. Something seems to go out of him, his shoulders sinking. He turns wearily toward the newcomer, CLIVE FINNEY.

                    NEWMAN
          Whatever you want, I can't do it. I can't help you
          communicate with your dead aunt. I can't tell you
          who will win the Superbowl. I don't do remote
          viewing so I couldn't tell you where your ex is or who
          she's sleeping with these days.

                    FINNEY
          No. But I've got a fancy black American Express card
          in my pocket—the one with no limit—and if you
          desperately needed to get my attention, if your life
          depended on it, you could turn it into the Queen of
          Spades. Like that.

          (snaps his fingers)

          You have a wonderful gift, Mr. Newman. And a
          terrible one. It's killing you. I can stop that. You don't
          have to be dead by forty... like all the others.

Now he's got Newman's attention.

>   NEWMAN
>   What do you mean... others?

Finney nods over his shoulder at a black Mercedes.

>   FINNEY
>   Why don't you let me drive you to your apartment
>   and I'll see if I can't answer that question... and maybe
>   a few others you might have. Sounds like you won't
>   be going anywhere in this.

Newman gives him a long appraising look, then slams the hood of his shabby Nissan.

7   INT. MERCEDES—DAY   7

Finney drives. The car glides over the streets like a shadow and makes just about as much noise. Newman turns his last check over and over in his hands.

>   FINNEY
>   You got let go.

>   NEWMAN
>   Yeah. Again. Yeah.

>   FINNEY
>   Wanna talk about it? About what happened?

Newman looks out the window.

FLASHBACK:

8   INT. GAME ON—DAY   8

Newman gets a puzzle down from behind the shelf and hands it to MRS. MCCARTNEY, a small and obese woman with a hard face. She wears a dusty, moth-eaten fox stole, the sort that still has the animal's head attached.

>   NEWMAN
>   Here you go, Mrs. McCartney, that'll be—

>   MRS. MCCARTNEY
>   This isn't what I ordered. You got my order wrong.

                                            (CONTINUED)

CONTINUED:

Newman frowns and checks a musty out-of-date computer.

    NEWMAN
  No, this is the puzzle you asked for.

    MRS. MCCARTNEY
  The one I ordered was twelve dollars,
  this is twenty. I'm not paying twenty
  dollars for this.

    NEWMAN
  It was twenty on the order form. I can't
  do anything about the price I'm afraid
  but—

    MRS. MCCARTNEY
  You can't do anything, you got that right.

Her voice is rising, becoming steadily more shrill. Newman puts the palm of his hand to his forehead, above his left eye.

    MRS. MCCARTNEY (CONT'D)
  I've never paid twenty dollars for a puzzle in my life
  and this isn't even the one I ordered. This is 4,000
  pieces. You know how much time I'd need to do all
  that? I should live so long!

Slamming the puzzle down. Things rattle. An hourglass falls over, strikes the floor, and smashes, spraying colored sand and shards of glass.

    MRS. MCCARTNEY (CONT'D)
  Not my fault! Don't think I'm paying for that either! This
  whole place is a damn maze of junk! You can't turn
  around in here without knocking something over! I
  think Jerry Abrams has arranged it that way! A person
  could get lost and die in this dusty little labyrinth!

    NEWMAN
  Ma'am, if you could just lower your voice—my head—

> MRS. MCCARTNEY
> Where is Jerry Abrams? Jerry? Jerry John Abrams!
> Did you put this imbecile up to this? Did you tell
> him to try and sell me a twenty dollar puzzle?
> *Jerry!*

This last shout is a piercing scream... undercut by a wolfish snarl. And all at once the head on her fox stole comes to life, twisting up, eyes flashing, jaws opening, and a dozen fine, delicate fangs fasten on her earlobe, and Mrs. McCartney screams and screams and Newman doubles over, hand clapped to his head, beginning to scream himself, his left hand shaking uncontrollably and—

SLAM BACK TO:

9   INT. THE MERCEDES—DAY   9

Newman lets out a long slow breath.

> NEWMAN
> No. Not really. Who are you?

> FINNEY
> Shouldn't you have asked that before you got in my
> car? Didn't your mama teach you not to accept rides
> from strangers? Clive Finney. I'm a recruitment officer
> for briteRside Development.

> NEWMAN
> The guys who made the chip in my cell phone?

> FINNEY
> We make chips in cell phones, refrigerators, ATMs,
> voting machines, in the last three security cameras we
> passed, and in most conventional spy satellites.

> NEWMAN
> What about unconventional spy satellites?

> FINNEY
> Especially those. Unconventional spy satellites are
> actually our core business.

(CONTINUED)

CONTINUED:

                              NEWMAN
Didn't you guys almost get bought out by Yahoo?

                              FINNEY
Other way around. Our newest frontier is implanting
chips in brain tissue, to ease epileptic seizures and to
help quadriplegics communicate. But we'll come back
to that. Your mother passed away in 2007. My
condolences, by the way. How much do you know
about when she was pregnant with you?

                              NEWMAN
I know she had trouble conceiving. There were a
couple miscarriages before me. I hope you're not
about to lay some *Rosemary's Baby* crap on me.

                              FINNEY
Your mother was selected to participate in a free
fertility treatment procedure, dubbed the Little
Miracles program, overseen by Doctor Eamon
Friedkin. About 1,100 children were conceived
through the Little Miracles, but the method never
saw a commercial release. Other, cheaper, more
reliable, and less controversial approaches beat it to
market.

                              NEWMAN
What was controversial about it?

                              FINNEY
It involved a crude early form of gene therapy that
may have accidentally sterilized an unlucky few.
Oops! There were some legal complications. Little
Miracles folded in 1996, and their research and assets
were purchased by briteRside in the sell-off. Follow-
up studies show that 99% of the Little Miracles have
gone to live normal, happy, healthy, and productive
lives. You probably see where this is going.

NEWMAN

I'm in the 1%.

FINNEY

Isn't that the American dream?

(smiles apologetically)

Eleven people out of the original Little Miracles pool
have presented with serious side effects. There are
some files in that briefcase at your knees if you want
the details.

Newman rustles out a stack of folders from the soft leather briefcase in
the footwell. He flops them on his thighs, opens the top one. We glimpse
photocopies of newspapers articles:

RAIN OF TOADS IN TOPEKA

LEVITATION OR HOAX?

LIGHTNING STRIKES: AGAIN AND AGAIN AND AGAIN!

BILL HOUSTON, 1980–2010; a troubled life ends tragically.

Newman drops the folder, goes on to the next one:

(CONTINUED)

CONTINUED:

MAN GROWS HORNS—DOCTORS PERTURBED

CAR MELTS—EXPERTS BAFFLED

PEGGY GRIFFIN, beloved wife and mother, dies at 25; Lovable eccentric with haunted past

And another:

IMPOSSIBLE LIGHTS IN SKIES

And another:

MAN FOUND DEAD, WRAPPED IN SPIDERWEBS!

And:

DEAD AT 31

And:

PASSES AWAY AT 27

And:

TRAGIC

BIZARRE

SUICIDE

DEAD

FATAL

DEAD

Newman shoves the folders to the floor, bites his thumbnail.

> NEWMAN
> They're all dead?

> FINNEY
> The ones we know about. We lost track of a couple.
> You've outlived all the others by at least five years.
> You're the lucky one.

> NEWMAN
> Yeah, I pulled the lever on the slot machine of life and
> it came up all cherries.

FINNEY

Have you ever heard of the quantum computer theory of the universe?

NEWMAN

I flunked out of art school.

FINNEY

I know.

NEWMAN

What else do you know about me?

FINNEY

Besides the fact that you wear size eleven Chuck Taylors, haven't seen a concert since Oasis broke up, and have been going to daily AA meetings since 2008? Not much.

NEWMAN

Quantum computer theory?

FINNEY

It's a fun little concept that's grown in popularity over the last decade among physicists and cosmologists.

The idea is that the whole universe is just an enormous computer, running a single program, which we interpret as existence. Everything we see and feel, the elements— oxygen, hydrogen—are just blocks of code. For reasons we haven't worked out yet, you can hack the system.

NEWMAN

What are you saying? I'm like Keeanu Reeves in that movie? Are you guys gonna show me how to slow down bullets?

FINNEY

I wish we could, but first we'd have to put you in conscious control of your own powers. You don't have much control, do you, Mr. Newman?

(CONTINUED)

CONTINUED:

> NEWMAN
>
> No. None.

> FINNEY
>
> And the sedatives... the psychotropic medications...

> NEWMAN
>
> They make him go away. Or they used to. For a while.

> FINNEY
>
> Him?

> NEWMAN
>
> Big Winner. When I was a kid, I had this imaginary
> friend called Big Winner. He was like my shadow,
> come to life. He was the one who fixed things for me.
> Whether I wanted them fixed or not. He seemed very
> real to me. For a long time. And the older I got, the
> worse he became. I never knew how far he'd go.

> FINNEY
>
> It's not like you—*he*—Big Winner—ever killed anyone.

Newman returns his gaze to the passing landscape. The Mercedes carries them past the athletic fields behind a high school, empty at the moment under a gray sky. Newman gazes bleakly at the abandoned track.

> NEWMAN
>
> Yeah. That's the one thing we both had in common.
> Neither of us had much ambition.

FLASHBACK:

10   EXT. QUARTERMASS FIELD—DAY   10

And we're in the past again, now in what looks to be the mid-nineties.

A meet is underway. Kids stretch out on the blacktop. Hurdles have been arranged along one length of track. Some seniors are performing the high jump.

A fifteen-year-old Newman is dressed to run, and wandering along the edge of the track with a chubby goth who might be his old pal Gerard.

Newman is making shy eyes at a leggy brunette, sitting on the bleachers with a friend. That might or might not be Susannah, now a senior. She looks back, gives him a crooked smile.

> GERARD
> You get one of those for me, man?

Newman carries two glass bottles of a drink called Smash!

> NEWMAN
> I was thinking Susannah looks thirsty.

> GERARD
> You inspire me.

An older boy thumps Newman, going past him. This kid, THE LEAPER, is stringy, pimpled, and pleased as hell with himself. Newman drops one of the bottles, which smashes on the track.

The Leaper has a crowd of awkward, acne-afflicted pals around him, including a thuggish dude in a Silverchair shirt. They glance back, but don't slow down.

> SILVERCHAIR FAN
> Get a grip, spaz.

> THE LEAPER
> Newman! Hey, Newman! Sorry about that. You need to wet your whistle, I got something for you right here.

The Leaper grabs his bag, blows Newman a kiss. The other kids laugh.

Susannah and the other girls over on the bleachers look away in embarrassment.

> GERARD
> Sorry, man.

> NEWMAN
> Forget it. Are they looking?

Newman crouches down to pick up pieces of broken glass.

> GERARD
> Yeah.

(CONTINUED)

CONTINUED:

NEWMAN
Christ. I could use a hole to jump into right now.

BIG WINNER
You aren't the one needs the hole.

He's just *there*—stepping out from behind Newman, from out of nowhere. He's grown-up too, Newman's height, but dressed for a funeral, in a suit and skinny tie. He's a hideous photo negative, flickering and bright, with those same terrible blue-white eyes. Gerard seems entirely unaware of his presence.

NEWMAN
No. No, don't.

GERARD

Don't what, man?

Across the field, The Leaper is preparing for the high jump. He makes his run, flings himself in the air and performs a fine Fosbury Flop over the pole. But the mat on the other side of the pole is gone and in its place is an open grave. How the—?!? He screams and drops into darkness. There's a headstone at one end of the hole and everything.

NEWMAN

No! *No!*

Big Winner grins. People run to the edge of the grave, drop to the ground, peering in. A girl stands dazed in front of the headstone:

DASHIELL FRANK

1980–1998

He flew high, then dropped within

Now he's gone—sucks to be him.

Newman grabs the shattered neck of his soda bottle and turns and stabs it at Big Winner. We pull in close as they wrestle frantically. Gerard begins screaming for help, and as we draw away again we see Newman is on the ground alone, slashing himself unconsciously while he struggles through a seizure.

11　　INT. MERCEDES—DAY　　　　　　　　　　　　　　11

Newman shuts his eyes and rests his forehead against the glass. He touches a hand to his temple. He's having a headache. He's always having a headache these days.

NEWMAN

You know I missed the last half of my senior year in high school?

FINNEY

After you had a seizure at a track meet.

NEWMAN

You know about the other kid? The high jump turned into a grave. I did that.

(CONTINUED)

CONTINUED:

                    FINNEY
And he climbed out five minutes later, unhurt.

                    NEWMAN
As long as you don't count a decade of psychological
treatment and a tendency to wet himself in public that
took him years to—

Finney laughs. Newman glares.

                    FINNEY
Sorry. I just think you're being a little hard on—

(stops—tries again)

The anomaly you're carrying in your brain seems to
be connected to an overdeveloped amygdala, a more
primitive part of the mind. The part of you that can
distort reality—Big Winner—is undoubtedly very Id
like. Compulsive. Childish. Prone to knee-jerk moral
judgments. Imagine him as a sort of negative image of
yourself.

Newman gives him a sharp look that Finney seems not to register.

                    FINNEY (CONT'D)
You seem like a basically decent, basically thoughtful
guy. Which means your Big Winner probably isn't,
unfortunately.

12   EXT. MERCEDES—CONTINUOUS   12

The Mercedes pulls into the parking lot of an economy apartment
building. What a dump.

Newman turns his Rubik's Cube over in his hands.

Clive Finney turns halfway around in his seat to face him.

                    FINNEY
You've had six jobs in four years. You don't have any
social life beyond AA meetings. I understand. You're
afraid to get close to people.

(beat)

You're buried in debt. Most of that is medical bills you
can't pay for a condition no one has been able to diagnose.

(beat)

Ten years ago, when you were working as a waiter, a
man's lobster came back to life and attacked him. Which
is pretty funny, when you think about it. Eight years
ago, a difficult landlord woke up in a bedroom with no
doors and windows. They had disappeared overnight. A
construction team needed a jackhammer to get him out.

Seven years ago you were working as a pool cleaner
and one of the pools turned to blood. Ew! Six years
ago, your girlfriend, Susannah, dropped out of the
relationship, and for weeks afterward—

                    NEWMAN
Yeah, I lived it, I don't need a refresher course.

                    FINNEY
Since the early onset of adolescence, you've been
warping reality on the fly, and while your condition
may seem like a curse to you, it sounds potentially
very lucrative to some folks at briteRside. You got
fired this afternoon? Great. Now you don't have to
quit. I'm here to offer you a nine-month residency at
our campus in Seattle. More than that—crucially—we
think we can offer you potentially life-saving
treatment for your condition. We've got an R&D
department for our most hush-hush projects, called
Darkside Development. They've been able to treat
people with serious epilepsy by implanting a chip that
normalizes the brain's electrical impulses. We think
we could use one of these chips, a Darkside Amplifier,
to bring your own seizures under control. In a worst-
case scenario, it does nothing. In the best case, it will
give you a new lease on life, and might just grant you
conscious control over your powers.

(beat)

                                        (CONTINUED)

CONTINUED:

All that and a ten thousand dollar a month salary, and
no obligation to stay after nine months.

NEWMAN

That's some offer.

FINNEY

There's a more detailed version of the proposal in my
briefcase. In the blue envelope. But those are the
broad strokes.

NEWMAN

And what does briteRside get out of this?

FINNEY

We don't know yet. Our Darkside team is in the
business of pure research. They're just dying to crack
open the watch and see how the gears fit together. In
this analogy, your skull is the watch.

NEWMAN

I got that.

FINNEY

The procedure to implant the chip is relatively low
risk, or at least as low risk as brain surgery gets.

NEWMAN

Would it really matter if it wasn't? I should already be dead.
That's why you showed me the other folders, isn't it? To
paint me in a corner? Let me know it's this or I'm all done?

Clive Finney folds his hands on his knee.

FINNEY

I showed you that in the spirit of putting all our cards
on the table.

NEWMAN

While you're showing me your cards, can I ask you
something else?

> FINNEY

Sure.

> NEWMAN

Did you do something to my car, so I'd have to take
this ride with you?

> FINNEY

Absolutely not. Although if I did, I might be reluctant to
say so. Big Winner might turn my next coffee into a cup
full of face-eating acid or something. Is that paranoid?

Newman snatches the big blue envelope out of the briefcase and half
opens his door.

> NEWMAN

It's smart. It's the first thing you've said that makes me
think you really do know what you're dealing with.

(pause)

Want to come in? I don't have anything to eat, but I
can make you a cup of tea.

Finney peers through his windshield, and grimaces.

> FINNEY

Maybe not. It's getting dark and you've got bats. They're
already diving your streetlamp. A bat flew into my face
while I was on my motorcycle once, when I was
nineteen, and nearly killed me. They've given me weak
knees ever since. Look the papers over. My contact info
is all there. I look forward to hearing from you, Brian.

Newman slams the car door. Finney watches him go.

> FINNEY (CONT'D)

(low voice)

You or Big Winner.

13   INT. NEWMAN'S APARTMENT—DUSK   13

Newman's apartment is so underfurnished, it resembles a monk's cell.
There is a single wicker wooden chair in the middle of the bare floor, next

(CONTINUED)

CONTINUED:

to a standing lamp, the only source of light in the room. Aside from a bookcase against one wall, there's hardly anything else. Some empty boxes of Chinese food on the window sill. Some empty orange pill bottles on the floor. AA's Big Book. The place has a cold, desolate feel.

Newman sits with the blue envelope resting on his thigh. He's working on his Rubik's Cube in a quiet, devoted sort of way. Something deeply unsettling is happening, though. As he rotates each side of the cube, that face turns black, until after four turns, he's holding a block as dark as polished obsidian.

He shuts his eyes, in obvious pain. Then he looks up, stares at the blue envelope. He's already made up his mind.

He gets up and carries his Rubik's Cube to the bookshelf and puts it down... with three dozen other black cubes just like it. Among the black boxes is a framed photo of a twentysomething Newman and his gal Susannah, in happier days. Although even here, her smile is fretful, her eyes are distracted; her man is very sick and she knows it. In the picture, Newman appears to have a bottle of beer in one hand, and his elbow up on a six-pack.

In the here and now, Newman's right hand shakes until he clenches it into a fist. He shuts his eyes and rests his forehead against the edge of a shelf.

FADE OUT:

ACT III

14   EXT. GAS STATION—NIGHT   14

Finney finishes pumping gas into his Benz, hangs the spigot back on the pump, and pokes his black American Express into the credit card slot. The digital readout bloops and tells him:

RJECTD TRY AGAIN

Finney frowns, slips the card back out and looks at it... then begins to smile.

It's sheer black on one side, but on the other it's a Queen of Spades.

Finney slips his cell phone out of his pocket, puts it to his ear.

> FINNEY
> Brian! I just got your message. So glad you'll be joining us at briteRside. Why don't we meet tomorrow at about ten and we'll go over some things?
> (pause)
> Yes. That's right. Yes. We can move forward as quickly as you want, we're glad to facilitate.
> (pause)
> Looking forward to it. I'll see you then. And Brian: you made the right choice.

He hangs up... then dials someone else.

> FINNEY (CONT'D)
> He swallowed the hook. Tell Mahorta. Oh and Burke... send someone back to the parking lot to remove whatever you put in his car to kill the engine. He sniffed that one out. I told you he would.

Turning his new playing card over and over in his hand.

15   EXT. BRITERSIDE CAMPUS—MORNING   15

The Benz rolls onto the green, oak-shaded grounds of briteRside Development (motto: look on the briteRside!). We could be visiting the campus of any billion-dollar tech firm: Google, Apple, Microsoft, Amazon. Everyone is young, dressed as if for classes at an Ivy League

(CONTINUED)

CONTINUED:

institution. The girls are pretty, floating along in skirts and sweaters from an Anthropologie sale; the guys have a good-humored, well-read, collegiate look. A few older fellows—Oxford professor types, complete with pipes and tweeds—wander among them, looking jolly and well fed.

The central building is a cathedral of glass and chrome and expensive landscaping. Blue flowers foam from the jacarandas along the footpaths.

> FINNEY (V.O.)
> We'll get you checked in and Doctor Mahorta will give you a physical and then I'll show you around. We've got you in a very nice cottage at the south end of the campus. Now we want to proceed methodically but if Doctor Mahorta likes what she sees on your MRI, we can go ahead with the operation in the next—

> NEWMAN (V.O.)
> I don't want to know. I just want you to do it.

> FINNEY (V.O.)
> I'm not sure it's strictly ethical to just wake you up one morning and say, *surprise!* We're going to cut into your brain today.

> NEWMAN (V.O.)
> And I'm not sure it's a good idea to give Big Winner a head's up you're about to put a leash on him. Just do it. Soon as you can.

The car glides to a stop on the cobblestone apron to one side of the central building.

16   INT. MERCEDES—MORNING   16

Finney turns to Newman, smiling admiringly.

> FINNEY
> You've really made up your mind. No second thoughts. No cold feet.

> NEWMAN
> What's the worst that could happen?

FINNEY

You could die under the knife. It's not likely. Doctor
Mahorta has the steadiest scalpel west of the Pecos, but—

NEWMAN

She's really going to use a scalpel?

FINNEY

I think it's a laser, but saying she has the steadiest
joystick west of the Pecos doesn't sound as good. Still.
Some things aren't brain surgery, but this actually is
brain surgery. I've told you the risk is low. I don't want
to pretend the risk is nonexistent.

NEWMAN

If you don't cut, I'm dead for sure. Besides... if you
guys kill me, you kill him, too. If I'm going down I'll
be dragging him with me.

(beat)

One way or another, he doesn't get to win this time.

17   INT. RECEPTION—MORNING   17

The marble floor is so polished, it looks as if they're walking across a
bottomless pool of black ice. The space is enormous, but not crowded.
Voices echo. Beams of gem-bright sunshine crisscross the vast, somewhat
chilly hall.

Finney leads Newman through metal detectors. Gates only admit them to
the interior after Finney puts his hand on a glowing plate—it reads his
palm—and speaks his name into a microphone, which confirms his
identity by analyzing his voice.

Guards in lightweight body armor nod as they pass through to the
reception desk. Newman glances at them dismissively.

NEWMAN

What are the requirements to get a security job here?

FINNEY

Military service, good marksmanship, EMT
certification. You have to look good in Kevlar

(CONTINUED)

CONTINUED:

> obviously. A lack of imagination and moral
> compunctions is also an asset. Bonus points if they
> can recite all of *Robocop* from memory.

They reach the desk, and Finney falls into small chat with one of the pretty ladies manning a computer that looks at least ten years ahead of the latest technology.

NEWMAN

Men's?

FINNEY

Two rights and a left.

Newman nods and wanders off.

18   INT. A MAZE OF QUIET CORRIDORS—MORNING   18

Newman exits the MEN'S room, drying his hands on a paper towel. He looks left, then right, and frowns. He doesn't remember how he got here.

He settles on a right and walks down a wide corridor, his Chuck Taylors scuffing softly on the marble. He comes to a T-shaped intersection, looks one way, looks the other—shit, he's completely lost. He takes another right, lowering his head and looking uneasily around, expecting someone to yell at him.

The sound of raised voices draws him around another corner.

A short hallway ends at a pair of doors. Some plastic plaques warn people away:

R&D MODULE 2 DARKSIDE UNIT

MINOTAUR CLEARANCE ONLY

NO PASS NO ENTRY

ALARM WILL SOUND IF DOOR IS OPENED

Two thin windows with chicken wire in them look into the room on the other side. That's where the commotion is coming from.

Newman checks to see if he's alone, then drifts forward to peer through one of the windows.

NEWMAN'S P.O.V.:

19   INT. R&D MODULE 2—CONTINUOUS   19

We look into a big office: desks, whiteboards, softly chirruping computers. The place is all but empty except for a handsome older man, disheveled, carrying a few cardboard boxes. He's being escorted out through a door on the far side of the room by a Robocop security detail, and a flushed, slick corporate stooge.

The older man, with his long graying hair and thick beard—I imagine him as Neil Gaiman*, possibly with the voice of Max Von Sydow—is DOCTOR EAMON FRIEDKIN. The stooge would be PAUL BURKE.

> **FRIEDKIN**
>
> What do you think you're going to accomplish by dismissing me? I'm telling you water is wet. Do you imagine, if you send me away, you no longer need fear drowning?

> **BURKE**
>
> We're not the ones drowning. *He* is. We're throwing him a life ring. Where's your empathy?

> **FRIEDKIN**
>
> No. You're throwing a match—at a stick of dynamite.

> **BURKE**
>
> If we were in the business of manufacturing mixed metaphors, we'd be offering you a promotion. But we're in the business of manufacturing the *future*, Doctor, and

(CONTINUED)

* As we went into production on the pilot, I asked Neil if he'd play Friedkin. He said "yes" right away. But "Black Box" was to be our second episode and we only ever filmed the first ("Sleepwalker" and "A Window Opens"). If there's one great disappointment in not getting to do the show, it's that I never got to cast Neil Gaiman as our benevolent Dr. Frankenstein.

CONTINUED:

> you're stuck in the past. Let's move it along. Your co-
> workers will be here in a few minutes and I'd like to
> avoid a scene in front of people who used to admire you.

Friedkin can see if he doesn't start moving, one of those guards will begin poking him with a rubber nightstick. He starts to turn away—then looks at *us*, catching sight of Newman through the window. His gaze despairs. He gives a quick, vigorous shake of the head that could mean any of a half-dozen different things.

FINNEY (O.S.)

> Hey, pard, you get lost?

20   INT. CORRIDOR—CONTINUOUS   20

And Newman jerks his face away from the glass, turning around, looking flustered and embarrassed. Finney, though, smiles hugely. He must know Newman just saw something he wasn't meant to witness, but you couldn't tell it from his warm, welcoming expression.

FINNEY

> Come on, I'd like to introduce you to Doctor Mahorta.

21   INT. FUTURISTIC EXAM ROOM—DAY   21

Newman wears a paper hospital gown and socks.

Doctor Mahorta leans against a nearby counter, leafing through a folder. She's pretty enough—striking enough—to be a professional model and there's nothing sensible about her heels.

NURSE MARTINGALE pumps a nylon cuff full of air, taking Newman's blood pressure. Our Nurse looks like an actual medical professional, not a Victoria's Secret girl dressed up as a doctor for Halloween.

MAHORTA

> I am so glad to meet you, Mr. Newman. You are my
> first.

NEWMAN

> I'm your first?

Mahorta looks up.

MAHORTA

First of the anomalies I've ever met in person. We were in talks with Rodney Houston—he was like you—when he died of an embolism. Terrific disappointment for the whole team.

NEWMAN

Not to mention Mr. Houston. And his family.

MAHORTA

He didn't have any family. Not alive anyway. They were struck by lightning.

NEWMAN

The... whole family?

MAHORTA

Yes, the mother and father both, and two grandparents. Not all at once. They were each struck at different times over about a decade. Naturally his nickname was Lightning Rod. Do you have any cute nicknames?

NEWMAN

Is that one of the questions on your chart?

MAHORTA

No. Sorry. Just wondering... what it must be like to be you. To have the key to God's control room. What I wouldn't give to have your brain.

NEWMAN

Yeah, well, don't take off with it while you've got my skull open. I'm still using it.

(CONTINUED)

CONTINUED:

Nurse Martingale laughs. Mahorta gives her a frigid glare.

MAHORTA
I think we're all set here, Ms. Martingale, thank you.

The nurse nods—abashed—and leaves. She shuts the door behind her. There's a mirror on it. Mahorta checks her make-up.

MAHORTA (CONT'D)
Too bad about Martingale. Your nurse? She wrote a brilliant paper when she was a post-doc, but she'll never be doing anything here except checking blood pressure and taking temperatures.

She glances at Newman in the mirror.

MAHORTA (CONT'D)
Average-looking girls never get the promotion, I don't care where you graduated in your class at Harvard Medical. You can only go as far as what you're born with.

(she turns)

Most of us, anyway, are stuck with the cards we drew at the beginning. In your case, though, I'm hoping to make your Joker into an Ace. Follow me, Mr. Newman.

22   INT. M.R.I. CHAMBER—DAY   22

Mahorta, Burke, and Finney watch through the glass as Nurse Martingale presses buttons on the side of the M.R.I. The steel gurney hums and slides into the glowing blue donut, carrying Newman in for a brain scan.

BURKE
He didn't even look at the consent form when he put his name on it. He signed every organ and every tissue in his body over to us for a lousy 90 gees. We could sell his brain off for a hundred million dollars a slice. What a chump.

FINNEY
What was Doctor Friedkin still doing here? I thought you were going to have him out of here last week.

                    BURKE

Someone on the inside let him in. He claimed he was
just collecting some things he forgot, but who knows
what he was really up to.

                    FINNEY

Newman saw him.

                    BURKE

What'd he see?

                    MAHORTA

I want to cut as soon as possible. Think he'd be all
right with next week?

                    FINNEY

I think he'd be all right with tomorrow.

                    BURKE

Suicidal ideation. That's part of the profile.

                    FINNEY

Yeah, that troubles me.

                    BURKE

Why? It makes it easier. Greases the ol' wheels,
Finney.

                    FINNEY

Well... the anomaly is under the power of his reptile
brain, his Id. He thinks of it as an imaginary frenemy,
nicknamed Big Winner. Big Winner is like his evil
twin, a kind of photo negative of Newman himself.
His opposite. So what's the opposite of the suicidal
urge?

                    BURKE

Joy, right?

                    MAHORTA

Or the desire to procreate.

                                        (CONTINUED)

CONTINUED:

> FINNEY
> Yeah? You ever think the flip side of suicide is homicide?
> That's why Newman is in such a rush to implant. He's
> scared. Not for himself. For us. He's scared Big Winner
> will lash out to protect himself and we'll be in the way.

> MAHORTA
> Oh, I hope so. Come on, Big Winner. Pop on out of
> Brian Newman's head and give mama a sloppy wet
> kiss. I want to date.

On the screen to Mahorta's left is a video of Newman's skull. It flickers, wavers, and for a moment we glimpse the grinning, death-face of Big Winner. None of them see, though—they're all staring through the window at Newman, inserted in the humming capsule of the M.R.I.

The picture on the monitor rolls and becomes a skull again.

FADE OUT:

ACT IV

23   INT. PREP WARD—DAY   23

Newman sits on a rolling gurney, a bit nicer than the sort of gurney you'd see in most city ERs. Nurse Martingale leans in from behind him, almost like a lover preparing to whisper sweet nothings.

> NURSE
> Are you ready for your haircut, Mr. Newman?

> NEWMAN
> Yeah. Just a little off the top.

> NURSE
> Will do.

She runs an electric trimmer and begins lopping his hair off in big soft wings. Newman's hair drifts gently to the floor.

Now Nurse Martingale is drawing on Newman's head with a Sharpie—circles inside of circles—while Mahorta sits beside Newman on his gurney. Newman fiddles absent-mindedly with a Rubik's Cube.

MAHORTA

The entire surgery will take less than three hours. You
will remain in the sterile theater, under sedation,
while we conduct start-up routines with the amplifier.

MAHORTA (CONT'D)
This will take an additional six to ten hours.

NEWMAN
Is that it? Can I see it?

Mahorta looks at him with interest, then gets up, and crosses the room to
a rolling table. Beneath a steel lid is a pit filled with dry ice. The Darkside
Amplifier nestles in the middle of those shavings of ice, stored in a glass
capsule.

We see it through the drifting smoke, a little disk of copper, etched with
electronic scrollwork. Why, it almost—

NEWMAN (CONT'D)
Looks like a penny.

(CONTINUED)

CONTINUED:

> MAHORTA
>
> A penny to buy a new life. A penny for your thoughts.

> NEWMAN
>
> You'd be overpaying.

They smile and for a moment Mahorta almost doesn't seem that bad.

> MAHORTA
>
> Are you ready?

> NEWMAN
>
> Let's do it.

24   INT. BUCK ROGERS OPERATING THEATER—DAY   24

Nurses wheel Newman into an awesomely futuristic operating theater, a brightly lit, sterile space, inside of a glass cube that brings to mind the Manhattan Apple store. Computer screens encircle his table.

He has an oxygen mask over his face. Nurse Martingale turns a valve on a tank. Other nurses, dressed as if they might come in contact with Ebola, check the monitors, prepare instruments. A tent is placed around the top of Newman's skull.

> MAHORTA
>
> Sleep, Mr. Newman. Perchance to dream.

Newman's eyes start to sink shut, then snap open.

> NEWMAN
>
> What if I have a nightmare and I can't wake up?

> MAHORTA
>
> No bad dreams tonight.

His eyes close.

Mahorta, behind the tent around Newman's skull, turns on a handsaw. It hums. The sound deepens to a painful whine as it encounters bone. Blood splatters her apron. A little squirts on a monitor right behind her.

A nurse moves in with a towel, wipes at the monitor and the picture loses focus and then sharpens and we're looking at—

A 1980S ERA TV SCREEN PLAYING "TALES FROM THE DARKSIDE"

25   INT. FAMILY DEN—NIGHT   25

Nine-year-old Brian Newman sits on the couch with nine-year-old Big Winner. They're watching "Word Processor of the Gods." Mahorta promised no bad dreams. It's a bad habit to make promises you can't keep.

> BIG WINNER
> I love this one. This episode. It's about a computer that can reprogram the world.
>
> (beat)
>
> You tried to kill me, Brian. With your pills and your drinking. You tried to kill me over and over. But I'm not going to let you get away with it. I'm not going to be your victim anymore.

                                                    ON THE TV:

Bruce Davison stabs at the "Execute" key on a smoking homemade computer.

> BRUCE DAVISON
> Execute, damnit, execute!

The screen reports: OVERLOAD OVERLOAD OVERLOAD.

26   INT. FAMILY DEN—NIGHT   26

We cut back to the boys on the couch... only they aren't boys anymore. Now a full-grown Brian Newman sits beside a full-grown and impeccably dressed Big Winner, that photo negative of a man. His eyes are blowtorch blue, literally: all hot blind glare.

> BIG WINNER
> The world should be more like television. More fair. More just. It should *make* sense. That's the world I want to live in. A world where people get what's coming to them.

ON THE TV:

Bruce Davison, who starred in the original "Word Processor," breaks character, turns, and impossibly stares right at us.

                                                    (CONTINUED)

CONTINUED:

> BRUCE DAVISON
>
> Starting with *you*.

And the picture vanishes into a single white line, which shrinks to a hot white dot.

27   INT. OPERATING THEATER—NIGHT   27

Mahorta turns a dial and switches off a monitor. Pulls down her paper mask. Almost no one else is around, and lights have been switched off along the outer perimeter of the theater.

Clive Finney, dressed in one of his dashing suits, rocks on his heels a few feet away.

> FINNEY
>
> I'm told the operation was completed in record time
> and that you're satisfied?

> MAHORTA
>
> I'll be satisfied when we know it's working. Ask me
> how I feel eight hours from now, when the start-up
> routines are complete, and he's conscious.

Finney wanders over to Newman's side, looks down at him—then narrows his eyes. A half-smile appears on his face. He picks a Rubik's Cube out of the sheets.

> FINNEY
>
> I never could figure these out.

> MAHORTA
>
> There are a relatively simple set of algorithms for
> solving those kinds of puzzles. Are you familiar
> with the concepts behind mathematical group
> theory?

> FINNEY
>
> Are you familiar with the concept behind "fun"? Have
> you ever had any?

She thinks about it.

MAHORTA

I had fun today. Cutting into Newman's Corpus
Callosum. It was like hiding a coin in a big quivering
mound of Jello. Or maybe... Spam.

FINNEY

I'm going home. Talking to you for too long always
makes me feel like I need to shower. Call me when he's
awake and ready to rewrite reality. I want him to change
history so Avery Babbage takes me to the prom. I can't
get over the feeling we were always meant to be together.

He puts the Rubik's Cube down on a tray by the bed and begins moving
away, Mahorta falling into step alongside him, leaving Newman alone in
the glass theater, under the watch of a few Robocops.

We close in on the Rubik's Cube beside the monitor. Every side is black.

FADE OUT:

ACT V

28   EXT. BRITERSIDE CAMPUS—DAY   28

Ominous clouds roll over the queerly desolate grounds.

29   INT. BUCK ROGERS OPERATING THEATER—CONTINUOUS   29

Two Robocops stand together, chatting in a desultory way. Behind them,
something is happening to the giant bright cube containing Newman. One
panel of glass flickers and turns as black and shiny as oil. No one notices.

ROBOCOP 1

Well I *liked* Chinese Democracy.

30   INT. GAME ON—LATE DAY   30

In his closet-sized office, Mr. Abrams buttons a shabby overcoat and
collects his ancient leather bag. The fluorescent lights flicker. A wind
buffets the building.

Abrams frowns and peers out his dirty little window—as a Darkside
Event descends on his world. Everything becomes a photo negative of
itself, except for Mr. Abrams. Although even he is not entirely unaffected.
His hair stirs, collecting static electricity.

(CONTINUED)

CONTINUED:

He recoils, lifting his hands as to cover his eyes. But then it's over, leaving him to wonder what he just saw.

He shakes his head and dips through the beaded curtain into

31   INT. A VAST LABYRINTH—ETERNITY   31

Abrams stands in a dim corridor with high wooden walls. Brian Newman stands on his left. Newman's hair is back and he's dressed in his usual shabby Army-Navy jacket. He looks as bewildered as his former boss.

NEWMAN

> Mr. Abrams?

ABRAMS

> Brian Newman? What are you doing here? What is this? What have you done?

NEWMAN

> I didn't—I don't—

The floor tilts and they stumble forward. Behind them they hear a deep, bassy rumbling sound. Newman looks back at *a giant silver ball bearing rolling toward them.*

Newman shoves Mr. Abrams forward. They make a right, then a left, descending deeper into the impossible maze under an empty black dead socket of a sky.

Abrams chucks his leather bag, getting rid of ballast. It hits Newman in the legs and he goes down and rolls onto his side and grimaces and—

—the ball bearing hits him with a wet squelch and he's gone. Abrams runs on, his panting breath rising to a shrill scream, turns a corner and finds himself in a dead end. He turns around but it's too late to choose a different path. He lifts one hand to hide his eyes, opens his mouth, and shrieks as the ball thunders down upon him and—

32   EXT. BRITERSIDE CAMPUS—DUSK   32

Wind blows. A couple walking under a tree cry out and run as a great oak bough cracks and falls. Dry leaves rush across empty parking lots.

33   INT. BUCK ROGERS OPERATING THEATER—CONTINUOUS   33

More panels have turned black, but the Robocops are looking at naked
women on a computer.

> ROBOCOP 2
> I like fake boobs because they're aspirational. We live
> in an aspirational society. All I'm saying.

34   INT. CLIVE FINNEY'S BATHROOM—DUSK   34

Finney turns the faucet in his shower, but the pipes make a squalling noise
and no water appears to be forthcoming. He frowns, adjusts the towel around
his waist... then looks at the lights, which are flickering and buzzing strangely.

He crosses the room, moves aside some wooden blinds to look outside as
a full-force Darkside Event crackles through the vicinity. Everything
becomes the photo negative of itself except for Finney.

(CONTINUED)

CONTINUED:

A glowing white form appears beside him, resolves into Brian Newman, who looks in good shape, even though we saw a five-ton ball bearing turn him into jam a minute ago. The Darkside Event buzzes and dies out, returning the world to apparent normalcy.

Newman now wears a terry-cloth robe and is gasping for breath, hand clasped to his heart. Finney observes him at last, and leaps a step back from him. They gape.

Back in the shower, neither of them sees the first bat pop out of the spigot and fall squirming to the floor of the tub.

> FINNEY
> Newman? What are you doing in my bathroom? How are you here?

> NEWMAN
> I should be dead! I just died! I was in a maze and—

Behind him another bat drops into the tub... and another. They're beginning to flap about and make shrill little piping sounds.

> NEWMAN (CONT'D)
> This can't be happening.

> FINNEY
> If it's not happening, then we're both imagining it. I better call Mahorta. I think we've got a real problem here. Christ, this is *bats*.

The high-pitched squeals of the bats in the shower cabinet draw their attention at last. The shower is full of them, hundreds of bats, whirling up into a kind of batnado. Finney wails with all the manly courage of Pee-Wee Herman getting his underwear snapped. He holds his hands up, palms out: *please, no!*

35   EXT. HANDSOME STUCCO HOUSE—CONTINUOUS   35

A high window explodes, as Newman and Finney are thrown through it, hit by a blast of thousands of bats, tossed as if by an explosion.

They strike the ground with a splat and a black crackle of energy. Newman vanishes. Finney remains, sprawled on his back, dead with his

eyes open. A bat climbs out of his open mouth. Viewers will be SO GLAD
they saw this moment. I trust they will treasure it always.

36   EXT. BRITERSIDE CAMPUS—NIGHT   36

A streetlamp explodes in a shower of sparks.

Two Robocops jump away from a security golf cart as the gale force wind
turns it over.

37   INT. BUCK ROGERS OPERATING THEATER—CONTINUOUS   37

One of the Robocops spins around and discovers the cube around
Newman has become a black block. They run toward where the
automatic sliding doors used to be, but no doors open.

The guards grab the glass panels, feeling for entry. One yells in horror; the
other screams. We see one of them—then the other—turning into black
glass. A hand turns to glossy black crystal, then an arm, then an entire
body. One of them tilts over and smashes to a few thousand pieces. One
of them remains, a piece of silently screaming black sculpture.

38   INT. DOCTOR MAHORTA'S PALATIAL OFFICE—CONTINUOUS   38

Doctor Mahorta stares into a vast mirror with a golden frame, doing her
eyes, while speaking into a bluetooth headset. She's dressed up in a
cocktail gown, ready for a night out.

(CONTINUED)

CONTINUED:

> MAHORTA
>
> Yes. Yes.
>
> (laughs sweetly)
>
> Have you been a good boy? Then we'll see.
>
> (beat)
>
> Now don't forget, I'm meeting shareholders on
> Wednesday, and I want you on best behavior. They're
> going to make some important choices about who—

The door opens behind her and Nurse Martingale peers in.

> NURSE
>
> Doctor? Mr. Burke told me to run and get you, but he
> wouldn't say what—

Mahorta covers the mouthpiece, turns and glares.

> MAHORTA
>
> —and I don't care, because I went home one hour
> ago, and Paul Burke is below my paygrade. For God's
> sake, Martingale, use one of those two PhD's to solve
> some problems for once.

Nurse Martingale retreats, shutting the door behind her. Mahorta starts
to turn back to the mirror... as a Darkside Event begins to flash around
her. The world goes black-on-white for a few moments, pulsing
erratically.

She hardly notices, distracted by a loud buzz and crackle in her earpiece
that causes her to flinch, shut her eyes, and yank it out.

The event is over in a moment.

> MAHORTA (CONT'D)
>
> What the hell?

Nothing. Silence.

She turns back to the mirror to hurriedly zip up her make-up bag, then
notices a weird white strand of hair curling from her eyebrow. She tugs at
it—and more crazed white hairs sprout around it. She covers her mouth

in horror... and when she lowers her hand, she's pulled her lips out of shape. They're too big and they're not centered properly anymore.

Mahorta opens her mouth to shriek, thoughtlessly touching her fingers to the sides of her nose, and bending it as if it were wax. Her nose is crooked and deformed now. Her teeth are snaggly and crooked.

She turns and runs through the doors, across a little reception area. She doesn't even see Newman sitting in a deep leather chair against the wall. Newman is shaken, smoothing his hands down over his chest, looking himself over. Like Mahorta, in her cocktail gown, he's dressed to go out in a handsome herringbone suit.

He sees her running past him, but doesn't catch a look at her face. He leaps up and gives chase.

> NEWMAN
> Doc! Doc, wait up! Something's gone wrong. I'm in
> trouble. I'm in awful trouble.

He catches up to her in a stairwell, which is where she wheels around to look back at him. Her face is comically distorted, the face of a troll out of a fairy tale: enormous beak of a nose, fangs protruding from beneath her thick lips, bulging eyes, wispy wild hair.

(CONTINUED)

CONTINUED:

Newman recoils in shock, wheels his arms for balance, and falls down the stairs. Thud, thud, thud—and then the wrenching crack of shattering bone. He winds up on the landing on his back, already dead, his mouth open as if to cry out.

There is a little photo-negative flicker—think of it as a kind of aftershock of the Darkside Event—and he's gone.

Mahorta walks down the steps on wobbly legs, sinks to her knees, smooths her hands over the place where Newman vanished, and for a moment it seems like she'll sob. Instead, though, she raises her voice in a gruesome choked howl.

                                                        FADE OUT.

ACT VI

39   INT. BEDROOM—NIGHT   39

A bedside clock reads 11:13. The phone chirps.

Eamon Friedkin lifts his head, switches on the light. His wife, a pretty woman of about fifty, peers at him with quiet speculation.

He answers the phone.

                    FRIEDKIN
          Friedkin here.

                    BURKE (ON THE PHONE)
          Doctor Friedkin. Sorry to call so late.

                    FRIEDKIN
          Hopefully you didn't wait until nearly midnight to tell
          me I forgot to turn in the key to my locker at the
          briteRside gym.

                    BURKE
          I called because it turns out water is wet.
          (shaky laugh)
          Can you get in here?

                    FRIEDKIN
          Within the hour.

He hangs up. Sharon Friedkin stares at him with a look of chilly displeasure.

> SHARON
>
> What is it, Eamon?

> FRIEDKIN
>
> They're in trouble. Einstein said God did not play dice
> with the universe. They *did*... and promptly threw
> snake eyes.

> SHARON
>
> They fired you. This isn't your problem.

> FRIEDKIN
>
> Of course it's my problem. If not for me, Brian
> Newman wouldn't exist. I'll have to answer for that
> now. I've always known I'd have to answer for it
> someday.

> SHARON
>
> I'm scared.

> FRIEDKIN
>
> Of course you are.

He kisses her eyelids.

> FRIEDKIN (CONT'D)
>
> You always were a sensible woman.

40   EXT. BRITERSIDE CAMPUS—NIGHT   40

Friedkin walks swiftly toward the reception area. Burke meets him in the courtyard, falls in beside him. A squad of Robocops escort them.

> BURKE
>
> We've got people dead. Finney threw himself out his
> bathroom window. Mahorta hung herself in a
> stairwell. Back-to-back suicides.

> FRIEDKIN
>
> Suicides, you think? We should be so lucky.

(CONTINUED)

CONTINUED:

> BURKE

Well, Mahorta left a note, anyway.

> FRIEDKIN

She did? What did it say?

> BURKE

"I am so ugly."

> FRIEDKIN

And... was she?

> BURKE

Huh? I mean—no.

(shakes his head to clear it)

We lost two security guards too.

> FRIEDKIN

How?

> BURKE

They tried to enter the surgical cube and—well—you'll see.

41   INT. BUCK ROGERS OPERATING THEATER—CONTINUOUS   41

They enter the operating theater. It is now dominated by a giant black glass cube. The facets revolve slowly, like a giant Rubik's Cube. A cordon has been set up around it.

Friedkin takes only a brief glance at the crystallized remains of the security guards. His interest is almost entirely invested in that big black box. He gazes upon it with wonder... and a certain admiration.

> BURKE

The first person to touch it was carbonized. It turned every cell in his body into crystal. We can't break through, or get any readings from inside. But we think the anomaly is still in there.

> FRIEDKIN

How I dislike that term. He has a name, Burke. Brian Ware Newman.

>   BURKE
> Yeah, well, we can't get in there and switch it off.
> Switch *him* off. We've shot it, hit it with high voltage,
> used a SWAT-grade battering ram. Nothing.
> (beat)
>
> So that's where we're at. The big question, the *only*
> question, is what are we going to do now?

Friedkin hardly seems to be listening, has the look of a man who has been both moved and inspired. He's already probably more in love with this cube than he ever was with his wife.

>   FRIEDKIN
> No, Mr. Burke. There's a much bigger question than
> that: what is *it* going to do?

And we draw away from the slowly revolving cube and the men gathered in terror and awe around it and then

                                        SLAM CUT TO:

CREDITS.

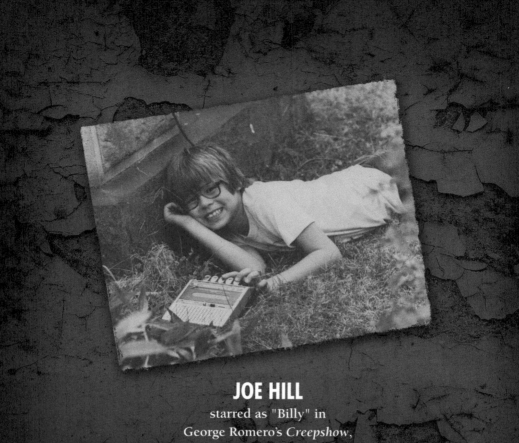

JOE HILL

starred as "Billy" in
George Romero's *Creepshow*,
under his stage name, Joe King.
The success of that movie
is widely acknowledged as
the inspiration for the original
Tales From the Darkside.
Having reached the pinnacle
of the acting profession
in his very first outing,
Hill retired from performance,
and is now a writer of novels, comics,
and unreleased television pilots.